PRAISE FOR
THE BALANCE TIPS

"Ambitious and brave, this book is a lyric meditation not just on identity, but authenticity, which for me is the Mt. Everest of oneness, you can see it from afar, but few ever get there. This book got me closer on my own journey."

—Jamie Ford, *New York Times* bestselling author
of *Hotel on the Corner of Bitter and Sweet*

"In *The Balance Tips*, Joy Huang-Iris writes about the spaces in between races, cultures, identities, histories, & also their endless points of intersection. This is a powerful & necessary novel about queer hapa identity that forces us to (re)consider the damage that has made us, the damage we create, & our inevitable negotiation with ourselves as members of the AAPI community. This is the mixed-race novel we all need in 2021."

—Jackson Bliss, author of *Counterfactual Love Stories & Other Experiments*, *Amnesia of June Bugs*, and *Dream Pop Origami*

THE BALANCE TIPS

JOY HUANG-IRIS

interlude press • new york

interlude press • new york

RESPECT AND GRATITUDE

To

Professor Crenshaw for her vital creation of
and scholarship on intersectionality

Grace Lee Boggs and James Boggs for their intersectional activism

humanity, resilience, and humans thriving above the systems/
policies that restrict equal access and opportunity

Alysia Constantine and found families

queerness, gaysians, and bi-bi girls!

learning, thinking, and living beyond binaries

the generations before me: Azou, Ama, and Ahyih

for Will, Barry, Kevin, Ma & Ba, Princess, Jesse, and Baobei

last but of course not least—for you, dear reader

AUTHOR'S NOTE

MY PARENTS TOLD ME THE earliest stories I remember. These are true stories, they said, part of your mother's Taiwanese family history; these throughlines are part of you, too. Most stories were tragic, violent, or both. At first, I didn't understand what domestic violence, military rule, and Confucian patriarchy meant, so I wasn't scared. My grandmother's, aunts', and mother's experiences were just facts expressed in narrative form.

"Your *ama* [grandmother] is naturally left-handed. The family thought this was bad luck, so her parents taught her to be right-handed. They used chopsticks to hit the knuckles and fingers of her left hand each time she tried to use it. Because society upheld being right-handed, and girls weren't to draw attention to themselves."

"Your *agong* [grandfather] arranged a marriage between your big aunt and his best friend's son. While *Agong* didn't know that the son was abusive, he later learned that his best friend did. But by then it was too late; your aunt had already married him and learned from experience. Still, it was her duty as daughter to uphold the arrangement."

Relatives expected me to nod and believe. And with each retelling, moral lessons emerged. I was a girl, and culturally, that was a failing from which I could never recover. Their stories taught me to fear, avoid, or obey men. To always protect the family standing over the self. Let filial piety guide you; your elders will always tell you the truth. And I listened wholeheartedly, at first.

But I learned that absolutes are rare. The truth can be not only slippery, but also contextually and culturally dependent. And even when an idea, mentality, or practice is widely accepted as the "norm," such acceptance doesn't mean we should forgo further examination.

I began writing *The Balance Tips* during my master's program. A year after I submitted 16,500 words for my dissertation, I finished the first draft. It was August 2016, three months before the election of the forty-fifth US president, long before the realities of COVID-19, and I was living in Seattle. While I let the draft sit, I took stock of the country in which I had been born. Current events centered on the flagrant murders and shootings of Black people, Indigenous people, and other people of color, some of whom were part of the greater LGBTQ+ community. I was horrified and constantly learning about the systems that condone police brutality, mass incarceration, and the funneling of toxic water to "marginalized communities." (Marginalized by whom? Pushed to the margins not by choice.) Whatever naïve beliefs I had held about the US were evaporating, and it was hard not to despair after the election, after the first hundred days, after the reports of immigrant families torn asunder and their children being housed in cages, after more fatal shootings and police abuses of power, after, after, after…

The United States is an ideal; we live in a country composed of various states, but the state of the union has been in crisis since white people treated Native and Black people with abhorrently inhumane, recursive violence. White supremacy, genocide, theft of lands, slavery, rape, torture, colorism, classism, capitalism, colonialism, colonization, xenophobia, imperialism, unethical experimentation, ableism, homophobia, transphobia, and eugenics enabled not just 1776, but where we are today. Our monumental wrongs, which we as a country still struggle to acknowledge and attempt to forget—which we have yet to take meaningful responsibility for—have in turn haunted each generation. The echoes of such traumas pass down as ghastly heirlooms. There has been too much assault, strife, and murder.

My here and now is 2021, and we have failed to follow through on foundational promises of liberation and justice. We have not given reparations to Black people, nor have we provided commensurate restitution to any group. Some of our representatives are trying to pass bills and policies to help, but often these efforts are blocked and end at "trying." And we keep adding to the already disgraceful bloodshed.

I cannot list the names of all the people whose lives have been unjustly abused or taken since I finished the first draft of this novel in August 2016. How many names are absent from our media? How many people are still missing, or their deaths unknown? The statistics are unending; numbers and names do not begin to encapsulate who these people were, what they wanted to pursue in this life, and who they loved and were loved by. Unjustly abused or taken. Because they were Black and/or Native, Asian, Brown, Muslim, Jewish, gender nonconforming, trans, queer, disabled, neurodiverse, an immigrant, undocumented, feminine, female, a BLM protester, a sex worker…ultimately, just *being* and *living* when someone decided they were not equally human and deserved violence or death.

After the Atlanta spa shootings in March 2021, more media/news outlets published articles and think pieces on anti-Asian sentiment and hate crimes. Why were Asian women targeted in these shootings? Was fetishization involved? What occurs at the intersection of Asian and woman? How could sex work or perceived sex work justify these murders? What effects did the forty-fifth president cause with rhetoric like the "China virus"? What about exclusion acts, and internment, and migrant workers? How has the model minority myth been used to criticize and gaslight other people of color—usually Black people?

People in my network reached out to me after the Atlanta shootings. How are you doing? Has everything been okay over by you? How are you feeling about that situation? Hope you are doing okay…

Truth is, nothing has felt okay for a long time. The more I learn about the atrocities committed in the US, the more unsure of myself and despairing I feel, despite years of therapy and self-work. But I have also (re)learned the power possible in positionality awareness, in seeking overlooked perspectives. My recurring comforts are reading and writing about the resilience of people. Even if my autodidactic actions are relatively small, they make me feel better informed and situated to support advocacy and activism. I am glad we are pursuing difficult, uncomfortable discussions about inequality, compliance, complicity, and accountability.

Because unearthing truths, upending silence, discussing traumatic experiences—i.e., reclaiming our narratives despite repercussions of "losing" face—these are acts of bravery and growth, not victimization and shame. Without self-reckoning, we fall short of healing our generational wounds, of addressing how we have been affected by intergenerational trauma.

I am the child of a Taiwanese immigrant mother and a white father whose family has been in the States for generations. Not only have I overheard anti-Black and anti-Brown rhetoric used in Asian and white communities in attempts to "justify" racism, I have experienced racism from both sides for being mixed—simultaneously too white or too Asian or too much of both. In hindsight, it is unsurprising that my racial reckoning took two decades. Coming out as queer and genderqueer took even longer. I had never felt safe to contemplate what "being myself" could entail, let alone how to support others in their identity journeys. I spent my childhood and young adulthood trying to survive personal traumas, afraid I would take my own life before age twenty-five. I made the mistake of folding into myself instead of recognizing how my threads wove into a greater tapestry.

By the time this novel is released, my thirtieth birthday will be fast approaching. I have learned a fair amount in the art of surviving. I want to pay forward the moral lessons from my own stories. To create a new narrative cycle, one free from the interdictions inherent in the stories my Taiwanese family passed down to me. I hold a different place in this lineage. I can think about choice, responsibility, and my role as "I." And I can offer stories beyond tragedy—I can create stories centered on the possibilities *after* trauma. I wrote this novel as a small contribution toward building a more just country and world. I wrote hoping to reach someone, to inspire and be found. As a child, I had scoured library shelves, desperate for non-white, "alternative" representation, hoping to recognize a potential version of myself between the borrowed pages of a book. I wrote for them. I wrote to offer alternatives; to imagine a self beyond the confines of the past. Of my past, of the assignment of cishetero womanhood—an assignment I learned to question, and upon recognizing myself as queer and genderqueer, to reject. And, selfishly, I wrote to soothe the most wounded parts of myself.

I did not write this novel knowing its publication would take place against the backdrop of a global pandemic, in this polarized, violent climate. Unfortunately, this has come to be. Despite appearances, capitalizing on book sales is not my aim. (Again, if my work reaches one person, I will have accomplished my small objective.) Instead, I hope this novel offers spaces for resonance and recognition, as well as opportunities for self-reflection and betterment. I hope we can remind ourselves to be kind to ourselves and others, and to strive for intersectional solidarity. With all this context, I now list content and potential trigger warnings for *The Balance Tips*.

Discussions of/characters' experiences with:

- homophobia
- biphobia
- anti-Black racism
- anti-Asian racism
- mental illness
- depression
- CPTSD/PTSD
- grief
- identity struggles
- intersectional misogyny
- Confucian patriarchy
- familial abuse and estrangement
- assault
- financial insecurity
- anti-immigration rhetoric

- internalized shame
- trauma, and
- bigotry

On a final note, despite what cancel culture argues, when we err, we are not canceled as people. We are not automatically, irrevocably bad or inhuman by dint of our mistakes. We can seek repair and we can (rare absolute incoming) always do better, so long as we listen and learn. We can revise our approaches "for betterment," as Ma would say. But we must actively make the choice to do better, to be better—all the time. Yes, we must try to make that choice daily, in every moment, especially knowing that despite our best intentions and efforts, we will have many flawed moments, many learning-curve moments.

To partially quote Grace Lee Boggs's sign-off,

In queerness, love, and struggle,

Joy Huang-Iris

RUPTURE

Northern California threw itself up. Yawning, shaking, rumbling. Upheaval. A battle fought between energy and plates. The ground rejected silence. Rejected stillness. *Listen*, it shouted. *I'm tired of holding this in.*

"...the Oakland A's take, take—holy—"

Static and snow swallowed the third game of the 1989 World Series. The television rocked twice before crashing into the coffee table.

As the ceiling lights broke free, pelting down, Jia and Hua Wu clutched at each other. Terror sealed their throats. Glasses fell, chairs rattled, shelves toppled. Books turned into projectiles. Hua ducked to avoid *An Introduction to the Law of Restitution*, pulling Jia down with her.

"*Jiu ming!*" Jia heard her own voice but failed to recognize it.

Ten seconds later, stillness.

TRIAGE

Jia

STANFORD'S EAST ASIA LIBRARY BEGGED for help. That's what Hua insisted.

"Volunteering is big in America. It's good. Come with me."

Hua left with staff members to recover the card catalog, which had endured a blast of water when a ceiling pipe burst. Jia watched her younger sister's back. Watched her walk away. Seven years since she'd seen that free stride. Since bowing to Father's deal. A price, an exchange. *Jiao huan*. Life for a life. She fingered the loose threads of the button-down she'd borrowed. Too much in these seven days. First flight and major earthquake. First time volunteering. In this two-month visit, what other firsts hid?

For a moment she stood, unraveling shirt threads, staring at the wreckage. Jia had never seen so many books strewn on a floor. Like spoiled children having tantrums.

"A sorry sight, isn't it?" a nearby male voice said.

Jia looked around. Busy volunteers paid no attention to her. No men nearby.

"It's like Mother Nature broke up with our libraries." The voice—American—came from behind her, but she only saw rows of empty shelves.

He chuckled. "Look to your right. No, your other right. Through the shelves."

Jia stood on her tiptoes. Between the shelving, a face. Wire-framed glasses. Startling green eyes. Feeling bold, she picked up a stack of books and walked to the other side. He was dark-haired, tall, and thin. Dressed in a fitted navy-blue suit. Smart-looking. Handsome, if he shaved his mustache.

"You work here?"

He finished shelving. "Years ago, when I did undergrad at Cardinal."

Da fei suo wen, she wanted to say. But she smiled and nodded.

He laughed. "My mistake, I should've said Stanford. Cardinal is its nickname." He offered to take her books, but she held onto them tighter.

"I want to try. Let me, show me how?" Jia wished she'd paid more attention during English class. Then she wouldn't have to speak like a child to maintain grammar.

Though his lips quirked, he indulged her request.

"Only a hundred thousand more books to go," he said when they went back for more of the fallen.

"Haha, you funny man."

He smiled briefly, a flash of white teeth. "Actually, I'm not joking. There are about 1.3 million books in Hoover Tower. It's estimated that ten percent were shaken down by the quake. We probably haven't reshelved thirty thousand, so I was being generous."

He led them to another empty bookshelf and they continued their newly formed routine. She passed volumes; he reshelved.

"You mathematician, Mr...?"

"How rude of me! Drew." He held out his hand, but when she stared, he dropped it. "I'm Drew Goodson. And no, I'm just a stockbroker visiting family. But you are, besides lovely, of course...?"

"I don't have English name."

"Tell me anyway. I grant you permission to yell at me if I butcher it."

"Wu is my family name. But you call me Jia."

Drew took the book she'd extended to him but didn't turn back to the shelves. "Jia," he repeated, extending the "ah" sound. "Nice ring to it. Does it mean something?"

Jia smiled shyly. "Home."

REQUISITION

HOW DO YOU COMPLETE A virtual application?

You scroll to the beginning. The mandatory fields are stars; their totality is your shining moment of acceptance or rejection. Cursor/ curse her, you enter: name, first and last. Forename. The name before the closer. What name do you lead with? The name your mother gave you when she looked down at/on you that first time. At your quivering small mass. At your blood-streaked skin, slick with her amniotic fluid.

Tomorrow will be the one day you could say, *I was born yesterday*— pity the paucity of your linguistic skills.

Mother looked down at/on you, and out it burst. The name to haunt you till death because you're too damned lazy to jump into the form-filling circus that's paired (with compliments, but pay here!) with every name change. Yeah, this name: Faith. A noun, a concept.

What's faith? Trust, belief. Have faith in me. Have Faith. What does *she* want Faith to be? So many possibilities. She, stewing in the sweat from hours of exertion, had no energy to imagine the specifics. How she, like your preschool comrades, would call you Fay. Cute then, cursed later. Too much rhymes with this diminutive. How she would stare at you when you ripped up the acceptance letter. Hands in white-peppered hair, her cry of despair. *Fay-ah, you turn down acceptance?* You scattered the pieces like ashes. And they are. Ashes of your old self.

Middle name, the intervening one. Stuck between first and last. Disregarded, forgotten, relegated to gasps while the other two breathe; it can forget itself. Sharing this name? This Wu, a relic of your mother's roots. The tenth most common Chinese name. Multiple meanings: military, business, affairs of men. Disclosure unnecessary. Without a mandate, you hide it.

Another asterisk. The digital star summons you to answer. Last name, sur(sir)name. What name do you close with? The name your father left you. This name can stand alone. Goodson. Son of Good? A Good Son? The original good son? What Ma would call *xiao zi*. Maybe that's why you're bad, with that hole between your legs, that hole between nose and chin. You can never be the good son, so how can you truly claim Goodson?

Down with the scroll.

What's your history? List in MM/DD/YY format.

Explain your experiences. Character limit: 2,000.

Are you legally authorized? (Refer to your origins.)

List your previous homes. Reasons for leaving.

Have you ever

lied under oath?

broken a promise?

pretended to be someone else?

committed a crime against your humanity?

succumbed to silence?

lost your mother's face?

If so, explain your decisions.

VOLUNTARY DISCLOSURE: SELF IDENTIFY

Please check boxes as necessary.

Gender: M or F (ERROR: no computing beyond the binary)

Sex: M or F (ERROR: no computing beyond the binary)

Orientation: N or S, E or W; straight, curly, or wavy (QUERY: bald)

Race: select one or more (ASSET: one soothes the system)

THE IRREPRESSIBLE
NATURE OF COCONUTS

FAY

AT THREE A.M., THEY RETURNED to Summer's studio apartment in Brooklyn.

While Summer took a shower, Fay stripped off her unicorn costume, trading it for the spare pajamas she kept at Summer's. By the time the sounds of flowing water ceased, Fay lay on her side, staring at the window's pale yellow drapes. She felt the queen-size bed dip. The smell of coconut shampoo, conditioner, and body lotion wafted toward her: Summer's favorite scent. Fay used to hate it, but now she never thought about Summer without thinking of coconuts. Or thought of coconuts without thinking of Summer.

"Psst. Fay."

Fay closed her eyes.

"Faker! You never fall asleep without a blanket. Why aren't you under the covers?"

Continuing to face the window, Fay replied, "Because I'm sweaty and I don't want to shower or grime up your sheets."

Summer poked her in the back. "So what? Come on under the covers where it's soft and warm."

"Nah."

Summer wriggled out from under the covers. "Fine. Then I'm going to complain about Theodore until you die of boredom."

"Try me."

"Can't you at least face the ceiling? I feel like you're turning your back on me."

Fay turned over and made a face. "You and your puns."

"Deny it all you want; I know you love them."

Arms behind her head, Fay stared up at the ceiling's glow-in-the-dark stars. "Teddy boy pick another fight?"

"He never does it on purpose."

"Teddy the instigator? Racist for no reason, then?"

Summer propped herself up on her side, facing Fay's profile. "He's just joking."

"Ha! But when Sophi and I joke about his eggplant-purple hair, or his colorful collection of skinny jeans, we're insulting him."

"Yes, that seems like a double standard. Admittedly, he's a little oversensitive."

"Your boyfriend lives for drama. Pity he can dish but can't take."

"Maybe. I blame his parents. He always got what he wanted by making a fuss."

"How much longer is he going to live in Mommy and Daddy's apartment?"

"Hey! At least he's passionate about Insert Label Here. He's always looking for gigs. A proactive musician."

"You know Sophi sings better. And she kicks ass at playing drums. *And* she has a real job."

"Working at the vinyl store is a real job!"

"A real, full-time job with a company that's not going to go bankrupt when vinyl goes out of style again."

"You can't compare the *NYT* with a record store." Summer sat up, crossing her legs. "And we all know how Sophi got the job."

"Her dad's an editor. He knows nothing about photography."

"Sure, but I'm just saying"—she poked Fay, harder this time—"that's an unfair comparison. Besides, at least Theodore takes me places. All Ben does is teach you how to mix drinks."

Fay glanced over at Summer. The city lights toyed with the shadows in the room, turning her skin paler than usual. "He's a bartender, what do you expect? And the diversion tactic isn't working. I know what's up. You don't want to admit that you can do better than CMT, so you're going to pick on my boyfriend instead."

"CMT?"

"Call-Me-Theodore. Sophi came up with it. You know, because he always introduces himself that way. 'Can I call you Ted?'" Fay sat up and lowered her voice.

"Oh no, not an impression."

"'No, man, call me Theodore. Ted's so childish, you know? It lacks the sophistication me and my band are going for. You should definitely come to our next show. I'm the *lead* singer. I can't play any instruments, but my angelic face (*ow naturel*) draws the crowds. Yeah, and the rest of the band is pretty good too. Ha. Aren't I so clever? Aren't you jealous of how hipster I am?' That's what he says in bed, right?"

"That's it. You so deserve this." Summer launched a wrestling attack.

Fay answered with a counterattack, and soon they were breathlessly wriggling around on the bed. "Okay," she panted. "Truce, truce!"

They lay facing each other, struggling to breathe.

"Stay still," Summer whispered. She used her thumbs to draw lines under Fay's lower lashes. "Your mascara's running."

Fay blamed the smell of coconut for what happened next. She reached out, drew Summer's face toward her own, and kissed her best friend. Summer froze, but then tentatively responded.

Jerking away, Fay shifted back to create space between them.

"Sorry. Clearly had too much to drink."

Summer giggled nervously. "It's okay. I mean, all girl friends make out at least once, right? And…and now we can authentically sing 'I Kissed a Girl'!"

"Totally." She looked over her shoulder at Summer's alarm clock. "It's five a.m. Better go to sleep now." She turned over to face the window.

"Um. Right. You'll get under the covers?"

"Nope."

"Okay…goodnight, then."

"Goodnight."

Fay relaxed when she felt Summer slide under the sheets. The covers safely divided them.

MATRYOSHKA:
RUSSIAN DOLLS

JIA

HERE, IN THIS ROOM, FACING each other. Drew's eyes reflect Jia's. Green beholds itself in brown; brown beholds itself in green. I see you and you see me, and I see you seeing me, and I see you seeing me see you. No windows in sight, but mirrors within mirrors within mirrors.

Mirrors encapsulating and transmitting. Projecting self and other, self as other, other as self. Mirrors echoing but also standing witness to this unbelievable transmutation. In this moment, we are our multilayered selves.

Under pressure, Jia realizes, education can fail. All time and effort to edify—to control—overturned. Names, facts, dates, equations, concepts: seemingly fallen from memory. Language shrivels into itself like faded blossoms. The mind reverts to earlier, visceral knowledge. But how is *this* sex? Jia only experienced the act once, a fast prodding with a cousin's friend. This, so different and unfamiliar. Every touch reverberating.

The thrill of exchanging the unspoken. The immediacy of perception. This dance, knowing no borderlines. Known by all humans, across villages, suburbs, towns, cities, states, countries, continents. Mapped or unmapped. At this bottom level, when every construct has been shaken, connection ascends, turns into the fixed point. Primordial communication.

This marks the spot where the road forks. The legs of the X meet to form a shared center. Here lies the crossing. Beyond is a passing over, a passing through.

No interlopers, no outside factors. No pedigree, no history, no past tense. Nothing but Present. Yes to here, now, this, us.

Time? A contrivance. Flick it off like a hanging eyelash. I hold out these hands, palms up. Place yours over mine. Palms to palms. Fingers to fingers, tips to tips. Wholly different prints, but here and now, my stamp is your stamp; yours is mine. See, feel how they fit? We meet in the middle and we match. Yin and yang, but with a blurred S.

Because we come together so smoothly there exists no intermediate. Light flows into dark like a tributary. Because there's no line between sky and earth. You can trace, but you cannot seize a skyline. It hangs, suspended breath, balancing.

Balancing on a tipping point. *This* is the tipping point. This is where gravity freezes. Where we float in space on earth. Beholden to nothing and no one. Let's. Let us. Let us be. Let us be alone. Let us be alone together.

Because here and now, here and now, our cells are on the same wavelength. The collision of plates, the race for rupture, for a break. Relief, expulsion is the end, but we delay. We stretch; we float. The day is long and the night is longer, and though we try, we know seizing this length is impossible.

When our skin bumps and our hairs rise, mingling like forest leaves, we think of love. We think of uttering this word that means, at once, everything and nothing. But if we utter it, if it builds in the chest, climbs up the throat, swells in the mouth, tumbles off the tongue…

If uttered, it is diminished. A bee releasing its last sting—finished.

We leave it unuttered. It levitates and we see its invisible presence. We feel its empty, full weight.

But in the silence, on our tipping point, it lives.

SLOW BOIL

HUA

SPICES, SAUCES, VEGETABLES, AND MEAT smothered Hua's countertops. Knives and spatulas and chopsticks and cutting boards fought for their share. Cookware and collection bowls commandeered all four burners. In the unlit oven, the sisters stored the food already prepared.

Hua kept pausing over the tea eggs to tell Jia where to find utensils. They spoke in Mandarin, but Hua interjected to quiz her sister on some English words.

"Strainer in the lower right drawer. What's a strainer do? Filter. On the second shelf, in the mid-sized pot. Careful with the lid—that's glass.

"Ladle in the upper drawer. No, it's not a spoon, it's a ladle. To ladle liquid. No one here says that; too archaic. You'd spoon the liquid. Yes, English is weird. Garlic press should be there too.

"Measuring spoons in the large colander, in the top cabinet. In the steel colander—the small one—you'll need to take down the whole stack of mixing bowls to reach it."

She expected her older sister to resist instruction, but Jia showed no signs of irritation. Her back looked like intersections of smooth lines. Hua stirred the eggs again, evenly dispersing them among the black tea bags. Lowering the flame, she turned to Jia and fully switched to Mandarin.

"You seem different."

"Hmm?"

"Stop—you can't open the pressure cooker. You'll set back the soup."

Jia withdrew her hand, instead reaching for the cooking timer. "Okay. Ten minutes left." She returned the jar of *la doubanjiang* to the rumbling refrigerator.

"More relaxed."

"The beef noodles?"

"No, you."

Shrugging, Jia scraped minced garlic off the cutting board into the wok. The pieces slid to the oil-slick bottom. When they'd browned, she added the long beans.

Hua stood back, avoiding a spit of oil.

"How're those classes?"

"Classes? Oh, the ESL. Great."

"That all you do?"

Jia scooped the gleaming green beans onto a serving dish. She appeared to miss the question.

"You go anywhere else? While I'm in class?"

Frowning, Jia picked up the plate of lumpia wrappers.

"You bought these!"

Hua waved away her accusatory tone. "No one has time to make wrappers from scratch. They're cheap at Asia Mart."

The cooking timer trilled, shimmying across the stove ledge. Jia caught the timer before it fell over. She pushed down the lever of the pressure cooker; it expelled steam in a slow hiss.

Clearing space on the counter, they began assembling lumpia. Plate next to plate, side by side, elbow to elbow, Hua and Jia built layers onto their wrappers. Smear of hoisin sauce, tablespoon of crushed peanuts, strips of omelet; sprinkling of turnip cubes, pork-loin strips, shredded cabbage.

Hua glanced at her sister. She was setting the kitchen table, arranging the serving dishes family style.

"But you're happy."

Jia switched to English. "What's happy got to do? Come *chi fan*, before it colds."

NOW YOU KNOW: A DOCUMENTARY, DIR. BY FAITH WU GOODSON (PART 1, DRAFT 2)

AUDIO TRANSCRIPT

Summer: Most hated dessert? Chocolate chip cookies. But I used to love them.

Fay: When did that change?

Summer: In the fifth grade. I come home from school. Key in the door. First thing I hear? Puccini's *Madama Butterfly*. Racist opera, but Mom liked the score.

("Humming Chorus," continuous)

I'm tears and snot. Mom turns down the music and ejects questions like a broken bag of marbles. She's noise; Dad's silence. I wish he'd had the day off. "Why the tears, baby? Talk to Mama. I can help." She leads me to the kitchen table. Offers brownies. Cookies. Opens Dad's pantry. Offers Pocky. Mochi. Like she can plug my tears with treats.

Fay: Does it work?

Summer: Of course. But it's a conditional exchange: one sweet for the whole story. I pick the roundest cookie, the biggest of the stack. Then I break it into bits. Two chocolate chips per piece. Like eyes. I eat one, sucking until they melt.

Mom pushes my plate closer. "Something at school?" I shake my head. "Someone?" I nod. Her name? Cindy Andrews. Has the look of a preteen Marilyn.

"What'd she say?" I eat another piece, wait for the eye-chips to liquefy. Nothing, I say.

"She did something?" Another piece; bittersweet set of eyes. I recall Cindy's smirk. The art teacher's back. The painting of Cio-Cio San. Cindy pointing, mouthing one word. *Slanty.*

I hold the cookie's end. Tears crawl into my mouth. Last set of eyes. Salt and chocolate mix.

Mom's waiting. With chocolate-smeared fingers, I pull back the skin at my temples. I pull until I can't see.

("Humming Chorus" cutting off)

(Exhaling)

HAVE YOU EATEN YET:
A PHONE CALL

FAY

JIA: *Ni chifan le ma?*

(Pause.)

JIA: No lie. No bother, I know you excuses. What you say this time? Same you always say: "Ma, just sit down to eat. Now you called." Right?

FAY: Actually—

JIA: Last week, you forget to call. How busy you are? Video editor, ah?

(Silence.)

JIA: You listening?

FAY: Yes.

JIA: What's that sound? No multitasking. Never do best when attention split. Saw study on *Nightline*: You perform at fifty percent less. Do you bad; you do this at work? I hear that! A voice. Someone there, you have company?

FAY: Of course not. I accidentally turned the television on; it's off now.

JIA: Treat me like your boss. No, better. I deserve better. You're so lucky; you only pick up phone and I'm here. What I do for *Nai nai*? Use Pincity for timed talk. And the connection! Sounds like raining

through phone. And *ai-yo*, poor *Nai nai*. So hard of hearing. I shout
so hard phone echoes. Like last night, I called, timer set for twenty
minutes. I ask her if she got the money. If she took it for the doctor
visit. Finally fit for those hearing aids, ah? You listening? Fay!

FAY: Ye—

JIA: I ask if she got the money, went to doctor. You know what she
says? *Shenme qian*? What money. I say—I wrote it here—31,759 NT.
Fay-ah, that's 1,000 US dollar. Half-half, from me and Hua. That sound
again. Someone else in your apartment? This a bad *time*?

FAY: Sorry, it's the TV again. Really off now.

JIA: No attention span. I never take long; you drag out by distracting
me. Where I left—yes, what money. I tell her how much and she *still*
forgets. Shame, so old. Brain failing her. I blame PBS. Should advertise
Brain Booster program sooner. *Nai nai* still be sharp.

FAY: Ma...

JIA: *Wei*, yes, I repeat. 63,519 NT. 2,000 US dollar.

FAY: You just doubled—

JIA: And she finally says ah, *na ge qian*, that money. Talking to *Nai nai*,
like catching a dragon tail! She says she gave money to *Gong gong* for
keeping. To *Gong gong*! Like she not one who handled the money all
their life. Like he won't lose it during mahjong! Like she has perfect
hearing. Fay-ah, I tell you...

FACING THE FORK

Jia

Late. By two weeks. This never happened. Jia retrieved the ticket, holding it in her hands like an incense stick. She felt tempted to bow, to pretend this god was *Zhusheng Niangniang*. But the Goddess only granted positive wishes.

The black details on the ticket seemed to dance before her, blending into the green borders. She blinked twice and they straightened out. BOARDING PASS. WU/JIA. FROM: San Francisco/SFO. TO: Taipei/TPE. 21DEC. FATE P4. She blinked again. GATE P4. SEAT 4A. BOARDING TIME 04:30. ZONE 1. CHINA AIRLINES.

Father's pockmarked face rose before her. Above her. Behind him, Mother turned her face away. No such option. Jia stared at the final destination. TO: Taipei/TPE.

Numbness drove her forward. She folded the ticket, barcode to border. In half. In quarters. Rip. She sprinkled the pieces, all at once, into the water. And flushed. The water churned round and round, sucking each piece beyond her reach.

SPOKEN IN THE DARK

FAY

INT. BASEMENT, LAUNDRY ROOM - NIGHT

BLACK. We hear the door to a washing machine shut. The machine is fed, change rolling down slots. The cycle is programmed in a series of beeps. Harsh lighting overtakes the blackness. Wide shot of LAUNDRY ROOM. Close-up of SOAPY, TWISTING CLOTHES. Continuous churning sounds.

> ANONYMOUS
> You'll black out my face and everything?

> FAY (O.S.)
> Yes, whatever makes you comfortable.

> ANONYMOUS
> What will you call me, in the
> identifying text?

> FAY (O.S.)
> Anonymous. Or you could select a
> pseudonym.

> ANONYMOUS
> Anything?

> FAY (O.S.)
> Anything.

> ANONYMOUS
> Jackie. Like Jackie O. You know she had
> some Black in her?

> FAY
> No.

> "JACKIE"
> Truth. Some Afro-Dutch blood. No one
> likes to talk about it.

FAY (O.S.)
Why do you think that is?

"JACKIE"
(Chuckles bitterly)
This is America.

FAY (O.S.)
Explain?

"JACKIE"
Well, you're not Blasian, but knowing
history, you can imagine. Being Black,
it's coded as an indelible stain.

Close-up of hardened GUM on floor tile.

"JACKIE"
Think about it. A *black* mark. It's a
reminder of America's "dark" past. A
black one, mixed with red. Slavery built
this country. But we hush it up. Kick
away the dirt. And I'm talking about
more than white people.

FAY (O.S.)
Passing, you mean?

"JACKIE"
Right, and general racebending/
whitewashing. Pandering to the ideals of
cisgendered straight white men.

Extreme close-up of "Jackie's" FOLDED HANDS.

FAY (O.S.)
How would you say this affected your
life?

"JACKIE"
(Laughs)
How hasn't it? I think a lot of it comes
down to appearance. How you appear to
others and how you want to appear. My
mom's Asian (Filipina) and my dad's
Black. He's a professor of political
science. Always been an intellectual—a

reader. Respected Black urban culture
but had no interest in following it.
Never followed Blaxploitation films,
Roots, or *Soul Train*. He was proud to be
Black and knew there were many different
ways to celebrate Blackness. But he
never had many Black friends. Everyone
called him an Oreo. Black outside, white
inside. Or a sellout.

> FAY (O.S.)
> But what do *you* think?

Close-up of "Jackie's" ARMS, transferring wet clothes
to DRYER.

> "JACKIE"
> I think that's just the way my dad
> is. There's too much posturing and
> performing, all in the name of rejecting
> supposed notions of whiteness. White
> people don't have the trademark on
> complexity. Neither do Black people, nor
> anyone else on the color-line spectrum.
> That's a human thing.

Echo of dryer door shutting.

> DISSOLVE.

CHARACTERS WRITTEN
ON NEWSPAPER SCRAPS

JIA

MY VISITOR VISA EXPIRES IN five months. The money I borrowed from Hua—she must know it's missing now; I'm sure she found my note—is running out.

I've been doing what they call in English "under-the-table" jobs. Sometimes working in laundromats, but mostly in kitchens. Working my way behind the scenes. Cleaning toilets. Washing dishes. Packing takeout orders. Food preparation. Sewing here and there.

When I finish at the restaurant, I work for the boss's wife. Babysitting. Grocery shopping. I sleep in closets. I sleep in storage units, head against bags of rice, body stretched across sacks of flour. Sometimes I live with women like me. At least five to a bed, we intertwine our limbs for warmth. March in this city makes me dream of hot Taiwan rain. But I curse these dreams. I call up the image of buckteeth, of meaty eyes, moon-cake belly, rod-like hands.

I feel like a Native. Hua had said Native people lived here first. The first, the true Americans. A nomadic people, like the mountain people in Taiwan. Before the white men arrived, Natives lived in tribes, following the migration patterns of stomping buffalo. Studied the land, the elements, to learn nature's harmony. To sing and dance her songs. Never cruel, never wasting. They killed clean. Used everything, like my people. I'd asked what happened to these wise ones, when the white men came. Same old Western story. Foreign devils happened. Foreign devils bringing war, disease, ideals of money and greed. These true Americans cried a trail of tears together. Unending loss.

Now I rub my belly, too tired to cry for others, let alone myself. This is my making. Each time I leave a heated apartment, my insides twist. I know the signs. That look in the boss's eye. Sometimes, even in front of the wife. Sooner than later, you pay for a free pass. Still, tempting to pretend otherwise.

But I know that's how it starts. Pretending, blindfolding yourself from the blade of reality. With no boundaries, no promises to myself, I could be like those other women. Taking chances with strangers. Following men into smoky, backlit rooms. Rooms thick with the scent of dust, of dirty fingers. Of greasy dollar bills. Price of necessity.

I'm too close to their level; I smell their misfortunes. Sorrow has a staying smell, many smells. Cigarette burns. Rotting, shredded skin. Pus and blood and urine and feces. They die ten thousand deaths before their final call comes. Do it, their eyes plead. We are envious of the roaches we share meals with. Exterminate to save.

I could become them. Without this other pulse inside of me, I *am* them.

THE MISINTERPRETED
AND THE MISSED

JIA

JIA FOUND THE DICTIONARY IN The Mysterious Bookshop on Warren Street. In a crate marked USED: HALF OFF. The communist-red cover, the way it took up so little space, reminded her. Of pictures. Of her father shouting, burning a pile of these *Quotation* books.

She brought it to the register. Unzipping her jacket, she fumbled for the uncontained change hiding in an inner pocket. The bookseller would see her money belt, would see it stretch across, underneath. Jia leaned forward when she heard the woman behind her sigh.

"Please, go before me," Jia said, stepping to the side.

The flame in her cheeks still high, she let everyone else pass. Finally, last in line became first. Peeking behind folds of hair, she placed the coins on the counter.

"Dear, keep your change. You look like you need every bit you can get. Don't we all?"

Jia tucked loose strands behind her ears, slowly lifted her gaze. Her fingers itched to touch, to cover the green-yellow circle under her eye. She resisted. Looked all the way up. An older woman smiled over chunky glasses. White teeth. Yellow headscarf. Dark skin and eyes, reminding her of the same complexion worn by Those Unforgettable Men. For a moment their voices filled her brain. *Outta the way—you know those fishy ch—that all you got?* Bile rose in Jia's throat. Pulsing skin, buzzing in her ears. She squeezed her eyes to mirror her fists. The flash faded.

"But...half off is two dollar?"

"Nobody's clamoring for that. It's been there for months. The strange bird of books." The bookseller paused, then nodded at Jia's stomach. "How far along?"

"How far?"

"Weeks in."

Instinct told her to take the book and run. Before the room spun again. But the woman's dark eyes demanded answers.

"Twenty-two."

"Ah." Her eyes rested on Jia's facial bruises. "And…do you need resources?"

"I fall and got hurt."

"Are you—"

"*Ni bu zhi dao*! No, I fall. Fine now. *Fine.*"

The bookseller paused, seemingly geared for more, before pushing the change back across the counter. "Come back anytime. Take care, now—of both of you."

Outside, the holes in Jia's jacket surrendered to the wind. The coins, still loose, felt heavier. With each step she took, they beat against her belly. An unseen, unheard beat. It matched the awakened, beating bruise. The memories intruded.

Who there? Get out so I can see you! On she walked, unobserving. Lost in the pain. Missing tourist traps. Street-cart sellers. Peanuts and dough. Oil and salt. Screech of wheels. She walked on, senses blunted, passing by the rush of city. Unseen and unheard. The Twin Towers, St. Paul's Churchyard. Click of Polaroids. Language collisions, vocal conquests. Liberty Plaza Park. Sneakers rolled. Dogs barked. Broadway. Unending shows. Sin is in! Glitter in grit. Heels snapped. The Stock Exchange. Briefcases, suits brushed. Registers chinged.

The unsaid. Shouted in the language of the body. Eyes. Mouth. Hands.

Victim. Target, written all over her?

"You look like you need every bit you can get—"

Your people sold you…

"You look like you need—"

We can do this civil…

White teeth. Dark skin and eyes.

"Every bit you can get—Like you need—"
I had dreams…
White teeth. Dark skin. Dark eyes.
"Every bit—You look—You need—"
smell of metal press of metal
Teach you not to mess with—
White teeth Dark skin Dark eyes.

With each forward step, her fear multiplied. Morphed into resentment. There were no kind acts. Only people wearing masks.

A MOMENT, DEFINED

Sophi: What didn't change when I came out? Coming out's a defining moment.

Fay: Say more about that. Your defining moment.

Sophi: (Laughing) Which one? I've got so many.

Fay: The first time something happened and you thought, "This'll change everything."

Sophi: My first kiss with a girl. Freshman year of college. Didn't even like her…too aggressive for me. But we kissed and I knew. The feelings I had—those would never go away. Being with a guy felt wrong for good reason. No denying it anymore, certainly not to myself.

Fay: How long did it take you to decide you needed to tell your parents?

Sophi: Since that kiss, I knew. I talked to people in the community. Wrote coming-out speeches. Looked up stories online. Set a deadline. But the more I researched, the more I pushed it back. Thought, next time I'm on break. The holidays? Terrible timing. Spring break? Too much homework. Summer? Too much time home.

Fay: And the more you researched, the more?

Sophi: Scared I got. You think of a million different ways to say it. A million different scenarios. You can only speculate on their reaction. My mom's conservative, but not as much as my dad. He's an InterVarsity minister. Worse, he's the East Coast director of AAM. Asian American Ministries, sorry. Telling him…

Fay: A daunting prospect.

Sophi: Yeah.

Fay: What made you afraid?

Sophi: The uncertainty of possibility. Possibilities. They could reject me. Disown me. Ban me from church. All those common endings.

Fay: How'd it play out?

Sophi: I wrote a speech and memorized it. Senior year, Thanksgiving break. When the relatives left, I helped them clean up. I forgot everything. Just blurted it out. I'm a lesbian! No segue. My mom dropped the pumpkin pie leftovers.

Fay: And your dad?

Sophi: Silence. Then he said he needed to pray and think.

DYSPHORIA |dis'fôrēə|

―――――――――――――――――――――――――――――

noun Psychiatry
a state of unease or generalized dissatisfaction with life.
The opposite of euphoria.
ORIGIN mid 19th cent.: from Greek *dusphoria*, from
dusphoros "hard to bear."

"EXCUSE ME. MIND IF I sit here? The other benches are filled."

A man. A pleasant voice. Jia gestured, continuing to read. "Feel free."

"Nice weather. For April."

"Mmm."

"What're you reading? Sorry, last question. I used to volunteer in a library."

She held up the cover: Merriam-Webster's *Concise English-Chinese Chinese-English Dictionary*.

"Long title for a short book."

This sounded like a joke. This required a nod, a smile, a laugh.

But then the voice registered—Stanford library man? Thumb holding her place, she rested the dictionary on her stomach. And looked for his face.

They stared at each other. Feeling the echo of multiple adjectives. Horrified, amazed, confused. And each derivative. All at once.

He spoke first, choking on words. "East Asia library...Stanford... after the quake. Wh—home...uh...is it...*Jia?*"

Noticing his encircled ring finger, she inclined her head. "Mr. Goodson. Looking professional. Still Wall Street man?"

"Yes. You, um, look..."

Jia turned to one of many folded pages. Too many folds: the upper corner of the book protruded.

sallow 1 |ˈsalō|
   adjective (sallower, sallowest)
   (of a person's face or complexion) of an unhealthy yellow
   or pale brown color.
   ORIGIN Old English *salo* *"dusky,"* of Germanic origin;
   related to Old Norse **sǫlr** *"yellow,"* from a base meaning
   "dirty."

"Sal-low."

Drew shifted on the bench. "Different."

She waited.

He swallowed, Adam's apple bobbing. "Pregnant?"

Jia nodded, closing the dictionary, and finally met those green eyes. They blinked behind the same glasses. She saw two sides, two halves of emotion. Half hope, half despair.

"Is it…?"

Nothing said it all.

RULED BY LAWS

JIA

jus soli | ˈyüs-ˈsō-ˌlē|
noun Law
a rule that the citizenship of a child is determined by the
place of its birth.
ORIGIN early 20th cent.: from Latin: *"right of soil."*
   cf. *jus sanguinis*

jus sanguinis | ˈsäŋ-gwə-nəs|
noun Law
a rule that a child's citizenship is determined by its
parents' citizenship.
ORIGIN early 20th cent.: from Latin: *"right of blood."*

IN THE WAITING ROOM, DREW held out his hands. She placed her
dictionary in them, bending and twisting to lower herself onto a seat.
When her breathing leveled, she edged all the way backward. Her belly
sagged between her legs to rest on the plastic. He settled next to her.

On his lap, underneath the dictionary, lay a stapled packet. In the
upper left-hand corner, Jia spotted a symbol. Inside the blue-bordered
circle, an eagle grasped a plant in one talon, and a mass of arrows in the
other. Pieces of the American flag were scattered on and around the
eagle. She tugged on the packet until Drew relinquished it.

Words arced above and below the eagle. DEPARTMENT OF
STATE. UNITED STATES OF AMERICA. Jia traced the circle. It
felt glossy. Below the symbol, she tried to read the sea of words.

FAM: ACQUISITION AND RETENTION OF US CITIZENSHIP
AND NATIONALITY

The caps made her sight swim.

"What's FAM? Family?"

Drew shook his head. "Foreign Affairs Manual. No need to worry about it."

She clung to the packet. "I want to see."

The introduction and numbered list seemed simple, but she failed to ingest them. Jia wanted to reach into the text, to push space between the lines. To transfer the sentences onto separate dishes. To cut the words into bites. No, more physical. Reading English could be like scaling two mountains, back to back. One: translation. Two: interpretation.

Drew eased her fingers away from the document. "Just focus on these two words: jus soli and jus sanguinis. Here, they're in your dictionary."

When she'd memorized the definitions, she closed her eyes. Lids drawn, overhead lights shut out. The darkness soothed. "What you tell your wife?"

"That I'm out with my brother."

"A brother?"

"Nelson." Drew paused. "From my mother's second marriage. Half brother."

The clock counted down to inducement. Fourteen minutes.

Jia uttered the ever-circling question as a statement. "What will happen to me. No country, no home."

"What do you mean? What about your acupuncture? You'll be certified."

She laughed, a song of dried leaves. "Certified to work without paper."

"I told you it'll be taken care of. Be patient."

"How? Why so secret? Even now?"

"Trust me, the less you know, the better. Just remember what you promised."

"You remember yours."

Drew muttered under his breath.

"Tell me. *To* me."

He turned. Those eyes cut like blades of grass. "Just pray the baby's not Black."

"*What?*"

He studied the tiled floor. Then he met her gaze. Behind those wired frames, green flames of defiance.

"I'm mixed. My dad's African American."

"Black American. From slaves."

"We're much more than that history. But yes."

She squeezed her eyes shut. *Hei wa wa.* A Black baby could shriek into her life. A forever reminder of that first encounter, intruding night. Of the bruise beneath her skin.

"You must tell me ending of your plan. Only fair."

"Anchor baby's a myth. Having an American-born child won't help you stay. Nelson's going to claim the baby."

"Last name?"

"Goodson-Bearing. Choose one."

Steeped in the worries of papers, legality, money, legitimacy, a way forward formed. "How your plan works? If it comes out?"

"Unlikely."

"But you say—"

"She'll only be a quarter. She'll pass, I'm sure of it. You just need to keep the faith."

AFTER THE BIRTH, THE NURSE left, clipboard in hand. Jia reclined on the hospital bed, holding her Asiatic-featured baby. *Bai.* Blank skin. She heard the nurse call for Mr. Goodson-Bearing.

Drew appeared in the doorway, a blond stranger trailing him.

"Sorry. The doctor must've written the wrong room."

But Drew approached Jia's bedside. He seemed about to speak. Then he stepped aside. The strange man took the space.

"Jia, how're you feeling?"

She stared at him. Fixed labels. White. Nelson. The father. The key. Jia held out their baby. He kissed the patina of hair.

The nurse looked from him to her, emitting a small "*Oh.*"

So much weight in such a little word.

FIT YOURSELF IN

FAY

SMASH CUT TO:

EXT. NEW YORK STREET - FENCE SITTERS, LGBTQIA+ Club - NIGHT

FAY, heavily made-up, scans perimeter, ducks inside.

The lit buildings of West Village New York are like glow sticks.

CUT TO:

INT. FENCE SITTERS - GROUND-FLOOR BAR - NIGHT

Full BAR, loud with chatter and upstairs music. Waiting in line, Fay watches relaxed patrons flirt. She orders a frozen margarita. The ASIAN GIRL behind the bar is her age. She sports a shaved head, has an eyebrow piercing, and is wearing cat-eye makeup. Her name is COCO.

Coco adds a CHERRY, pressing it into the drink's slushy center. Fay and Coco exchange smiles. Fay takes the glass by its neck and heads to a corner. Glances back at Coco. She's watching her.

DISSOLVE TO:

INT. COCO'S APARTMENT - BEDROOM - MORNING

Silence. Fay rolls out of BED. Picks up her clothes. Goes to the bathroom. Returns to find Coco sitting up. Apology on her face, Fay leans over for a kiss.

                    COCO
        See you around. No hard feelings.

A BOXED LIFE

HUA STUCK HER FOOT IN the door. Through the crack escaped the scent of overripe bananas.

"You're going to let me in." She switched to Mandarin and repeated the statement. "She's looking at us. You want her to remember this?"

The pushing stopped, the door dropped.

Hua caught it before it slammed, following Jia inside.

"Already so tall! Hi, treasured one, I'm your auntie. Auntie Hua."

"Hands off! Strangers make her cry."

"Oh? Whose fault is that?"

Jia seemed to bite back a retort. She pivoted on her heel, already traversing the space separating the entryway from the kitchen.

Thirty seconds of scanning and Hua drew all necessary visual conclusions. It only *looked* like the walls were closing in. A ninety-square-foot box. Ninety square feet housed the lives of her niece and older sister.

You stepped in, turned right and your hips crashed into the countertop, your feet into the mini fridge. The square sink couldn't contain a watermelon. Certainly too small to wash a toddler. Above the faucet spout, a shelf on which a microwave perched. Beside the microwave were spices, loose fruit, canned beans, stacked toiletries. On the next level up, two cabinets. Atop them sat a washbasin and a laundry basket.

Cracked plaster for walls. No separation between the distinct spheres of domestic space. Hanging from a rod: pots, pans, cutting boards, spatulas, dish and paper towels. Next to the rod, the smoke detector. Below that, a warped mirror. Above that, a Chinese banner: the character for luck. Then two hanging folding chairs. Wedged under those, a collapsible table.

Two more steps and you reached the twin-size bed. On it, between the pillows, reclined a Qing Dynasty doll. You needed to climb over the bed, ducking the hanging lamp, to reach the stuffed, skinny bookshelf. A radiator stood on the bottom shelf. To its right, a surprise: a French window. You could sit on its wide ledge and read under the sun.

Or you could sit with your back against the panes, see the opposite wall. The shelf and atop it, the radio. Underneath that, the bureau, on which acupuncture and massage therapy books were piled high. Next to the bureau, against this wall, a multipurpose ladder. A plastic stool that the girl toddler sat on, watching you inspect the room. To her right, a shoe rack, double shoe pairs in each compartment: one big pair, one small.

The final component, or the first if you opened the door and looked left: a makeshift walk-in closet. Three pipes jutted out from the wall. From the two outer pipes hung women's clothes; from the middle pipe, toddler's clothes. Beneath, brown bags contained folded plastic ones.

"Where do you keep your cutlery?"

"Upper drawer under the sink."

"Your garbage?"

"Lower drawer under the sink."

"That doesn't look like it opens."

"It's built off track. At the same time you have to kick it and jerk it open."

"Jia. Stop running from me. I'm teaching here, tenure track. Let me help."

"No."

"Why fight me? What've I done to deserve this?"

Silence.

"You've changed so much."

"Little sister, change is life. Life is change."

"Jia. Do you blame me? Why do I feel…it's like there's a world between us."

Silence.

Hua swept out her arms. "You think *this* is a viable way to live? Forget about yourself. You think it's healthy to raise a *child* in a…a cubicle?"

"It's better than a cubicle. You obviously never saw 81 Bowery. Sixty-four square feet."

"Where's your bathroom?"

"Down the hall. We share with two other tenants."

"You go with her to the bathroom?"

"Yes."

"*Every* time?"

"I refuse to answer stupid questions. I'm a good mother."

Jia stuck out her chin, daring Hua to challenge her.

The toddler stood up, pushing the stool as close to the wall as possible. She teetered over and stood next to her mother's legs— without touching them. Eyes wide, she appeared to assess this new adult.

Hua deflated. "Just the two of you?"

A pause worth a blink. "Yes."

MIMESIS

HUA

HUA SMILED AT HER NIECE. Her best student; a testament to the flexibility of youth. The trustworthiness of innocence.

"*Xin xin*, Fay. Mandarin first, then English. Remember, too, the hand motions. Start with "*Datou,*" big head; end with "*Ni Wa Wa,*" the doll of clay."

"That's right! Just slow your pace. How about *buh puh muh fuh*? And the ABCs?"

"Good! *Wo zhi dao ni yao*, I know you want. Relax, Ma comes home any minute now. Help *Ayi*, Auntie clean up?"

After tucking Fay in for the night, Hua and Jia drew the translucent curtain across the room. They took cups of jasmine tea to the door, orienting their chairs toward Fay's rising and falling chest.

Watching her niece, Hua smiled. "We'll raise her to have a round head. With the love and understanding we always wanted."

Jia blew on her tea. Too hard: some slopped over the rim, spattering her housedress.

"I'm glad you had a daughter."

"Why? So she can have a life of pain?" Jia rose to wet a towel.

"Bad day at work, then?"

Her sister seemed to dedicate all attention to rubbing out the stains. But Hua felt those waves of resentment. They were strongest in silence.

Hua brought her cup to the sink. Exchanged slippers for shoes, lifted her coat from a door hook, and turned with coat in hand. "I should go."

Then, softly, like feathers grazing skin: "Father and I. We had a deal."

Returning to the empty seat, Hua laid the coat across her lap. And waited.

Jia switched to Taiwanese to release her deluge.

"What's in a name? Do you remember, Hua, or are you too American now? Yours, flower. Mine, home. Fay's, conviction. We push all our hopes into names. Hoping they'll be fulfilled. Thinking them positive expectations. Wrong! Names restrain, lock. Locked in, locked out, locked up, locked down. Too much pressure. We shake under it. We'll break. Maybe not now, today, or tomorrow. Or even the next year, next decade. But sometime. If the earth can buckle into itself, we can too. Our bodies are too small to stand strain. We doubly react to the clashing of inner plates.

"When we erupt, splitting open, there's no easy sewing job. The stench of wounds lingers. Poisons thoughts, the senses. Blame solidifies. For years I tried to maintain hating you. Stored my resentment, trying to mold it into hate. You, Ba's and Ma's favorite. Smart enough to be a boy. Raised to be the boy. Worse, also with classical aristocratic features that made the women suck their teeth with envy. You, meeting, then floating above pressure. The heavier the ghosts, the surer you invoked the names of their vanquishers.

"I failed to hate you. Somehow you never forgot me. Always fought to include me. Like the Goddess of Mercy, you Perceive the Cries of the World. I kept my churnings inside. You could be the honored one. I strove to be the filial elder sister. The self-abnegating daughter. Remember when I stayed with Auntie for a year, learning massage from the Buddhist nuns? I tried to kill the desire inside me. She tried to help. But my will, my desire for desire fought to live.

"Think of this, little Hua. Two girls. If one becomes honorary boy, masculine sun of life, *yang*, the other must be ten thousand times *yin*. Ten thousand times passive, sustaining. Ten thousand times solid, cold earth. I knew this without being told. And still they told me. The firstborn! Every minute. Every day. Ba and Ma, all aunties and uncles and cousins and grandparents. After every exam you soared through. I may be born first, but born an ordinary girl. Know my place at the bottom. If you glided to America, my already folded wings needed to be clipped. Even without politics, I'm sure Ba would've promised me. One leaves to live, the other stays to pay the difference. Balance. Life for a life."

CENTER OF THE SNARE

FADE IN:

**INT. WEST VILLAGE, NEW YORK - FAY'S 90-SQ-FT APT
- AFTERNOON**

Fay sets the opened folding table. Moves the TWO BOWLS
so they line up opposite one another. Places CHOPSTICKS
on HOLDERS to right of each bowl.

> JIA (O.S.)
> (Knocks)
> Fay-ah, let me in.

Looking up, Fay straightens and evens chopsticks.

> FAY
> It's open.

Jia steps inside, shutting the door. Putting Chinese
GROCERY BAGS on the ground, she turns the DEADBOLT,
fastens the CHAIN, and sets the code.

> JIA
> You left it open? I could be anybody!

> FAY
> But you're not.

> JIA
> *Fei hua.* Foolish talk.

> FAY
> No need to translate.

> JIA
> No use you lose.

Fay retrieves bags, bringing them over to the KITCHEN.
While Jia inspects the apartment, moving things as she

sees fit, Fay takes out TUPPERWARE CONTAINERS. She keeps reaching—more Tupperware than she'd expected.

> FAY
> Could you stop moving things?

> JIA
> Fixing. Making better.

> FAY
> No. Then I waste time searching for what I need. Last month it took me thirty minutes to find my USB. I left it on the table for good reason. (Mutters) Who hides a USB in a red envelope?

> JIA
> No robber looks for *hongbao*.

CUT TO:

INT. FAY'S 90-SQ-FT APT - KITCHEN/DINING/LIVING ROOM - AFTERNOON

Fay and Jia eat, CHOPSTICKS clinking against bowls. Every so often Jia uses her chopsticks to place a bite of food in Fay's bowl. Fay moves these additions to one side of her bowl, eating from her own selections (on the other side). Jia's additions are in danger of spilling over. Otherwise, their attention is trained on the TV. *Animal Planet* features a program on Jane Goodall. Onscreen is a GORILLA, caught in a snare.

> JIA
> (Pointing chopsticks in
> direction of screen)
> Black people think we under them.

> FAY
> I'm sorry?

> JIA
> No blame on you.

> FAY
> You misunderstand.

                    JIA
Obama. *Hei ren.* So popular in culture.
No room for us. No room but silence. But
what they are, really?

Gorilla roars, struggling to free itself. Fay stops
eating, stares at her mother.

                    FAY
You mean *who* are they. They're *people.*

                    JIA
No hard work. No class. No evolution.

                    FAY
Where did you learn this anti-Black
racist shit? American media?

                    JIA
No curses. What racist? I can't be. An
immigrant, I came here—

               FAY
          (Putting up a hand)
Please check yourself. How many times
do we have to tell you? Everyone can be
racist, can spout anti-Black bullshit—
fine, BS. You wanna be that person? A
puppet for white supremacy?

               JIA
          (Plucking a slice of beef
          and placing it in Fay's
          bowl)
No, *you* listen. We have a saying. "A
girl can be ugly, as long as she has
white skin."

               FAY
We have a saying, check your privilege!
Where's your empathy? Look up "history"
in that dictionary of yours! Look up
imperialism, colonization, genocide,
slavery, murder, rape, misogyny, abuse,
colorism, robbery of rights—

                              JIA
          Robbery? ROBBERY? *Bi zui*!

                              FAY
          Shut up? *You're* the one always telling
          me to speak my mind, are you the
          exception—

                              JIA
          Robbery. (Disbelieving, voice trembling)
          Robbery. Ungrateful!

                              FAY
          How am *I* un—

                              JIA
          Case close! Shut *fuck* up! *Fu xin*, where
          your loyalty I gave you my—shut up SHUT
          UP *BI ZUI*!

Fay stabs CHOPSTICKS into the mound of RICE centered in
her bowl. Scraping her chair backward, she relocates
to her bed. Onscreen, coaxing researchers approach the
furious gorilla. Fay increases the volume to antagonize
her mother. But the unity of visual and aural cacophony
bothers Fay more. Jia removes the upright chopsticks
and hurls them across the room as a tan woman—hidden by
fronds—shoots the gorilla with a tranquilizer gun.

CODES WE EAT

Fay

FADE IN:

INT. COLUMBIA UNIVERSITY, HUMANITIES OFFICE - DAY

Wide shot of OFFICE. Pan from filing cabinets to paper
mounds, turgid bookshelves, orphan coffee cups.

> PROFESSOR YI (O.S.)
> I identify as a second-generation
> American. After my parents immigrated to
> the Bay Area—due to job offers—they had
> me. But they never taught me Chinese.
> Wanted me to have perfect English.

Extreme close-up of EXTENDED-FAMILY PICTURE on
Professor Yi's desk.

> FAY (O.S.)
> What were their occupations?

> PROFESSOR YI
> They were scientists.

> FAY (O.S.)
> Did they expect you to enter a similar
> field?

> PROFESSOR YI
> Yes and no. I've always been adept at
> math and science, but they knew I didn't
> find it interesting. So they encouraged
> me to explore. At UC Berkeley, I took
> Asian-American Anthropology. And that
> sealed my fate.

Close-up of UC Berkeley DIPLOMA.

> FAY (O.S.)
> Favorite class to teach?

PROFESSOR YI
Easy choice. Etiquette and Customs in
Chinese Dining. (Laughs) Yes, that's
typically the reaction I receive from
students. But they quickly realize how
fascinating these protocols are. I teach
more than the rules. I reveal the "why"
behind the whimsy.

FAY (O.S.)
Like why we're taught to handle
chopsticks in certain ways?

PROFESSOR YI
Exactly. In fact, let me display my
demonstration kit.

Mid-shot of Chinese PLACE SETTING.

FAY (O.S.)
My mother would tell me, "Never do [X or
Y]," but never explain.

PROFESSOR YI
Most cultural codes and norms are taught
that way. It's like learning a dance
without purpose. Since you brought up
chopsticks, let's unpack this aspect of
etiquette.

Switch to Professor Yi's V.O.; pair with DEMO of faux
pas.

Afterward, FADE OUT to erhu music.

TOP TEN
CHOPSTICK FAUX PAS

1. Setting down chopsticks unevenly

   Reasoning behind interdiction: *san chang liang duan,* "three long and two short." Traditionally, the dead were placed in coffins made of uneven boards (long boards composed the sides and bottom; short boards composed the front and back).

2. Pointing with chopsticks

   Reasoning: this indicates abuse because the Chinese point at others while scolding.

3. Sticking upright chopsticks in dishes

   Reasoning: positioning chopsticks in this manner resembles the positioning of incense sticks. When offering sacrifices to the dead, worshippers insert incense into a burner's center.

4. Excavating food with chopsticks

   Reasoning: a rude action that's also inauspicious; some call this "grave-digging."

5. Drumming crockery with chopsticks

   Reasoning: using chopsticks as noisemakers harks back to street begging.

6. Sucking on chopsticks (audibly)

   Reasoning: this implies immaturity, poor education, or "low-class" status, which shames your parents.

7. Spearing food with chopsticks

   Reasoning: same as previous, except now this also indicates foreignness.

8. Reversing Heaven and Earth

   Reasoning: placing chopsticks upside down upsets balance; it's like placing a baby on its head.

9. Crisscrossing chopsticks

   Reasoning: this "X" sign negates those eating around you, especially the host. Furthermore, the cross is reminiscent of a signature—like the signature required after being charged and writing a confession.

10. Dropping chopsticks on the ground

    Reasoning: such a mistake is arguably the most taboo. Because all people used to be buried, the Chinese feel that dropped chopsticks disturb their ancestors. Interestingly, there's a way of "undoing" this. The transgressor must pick up the fallen chopsticks and cross them east to west, and then north to south. Bonus points if they mutter "I'm a damn fool" while doing so.

DROP OF BLOOD

JIA

"MA, *NI KAN, KAN*! LOOK, look!"

Jia closed the dictionary. Her daughter bounded onto the bench, pressing a squishy blob into her hands.

"What is this?" She responded as planned: in Mandarin. Hua spoke the English. Fay needed to speak in both tongues, one after another.

Her daughter pointed. The thing meant to speak for itself. But in the transference it'd been unmolded.

"*Ni wa wa.* The doll of clay."

"This all you do at kindergarten? Shape clay?"

"*Women ye hua hua.* We painted too!"

"Come on, let's go home."

Only when they put on their house slippers did she see it.

"What's that on your face?"

"*Bu zhi dao.* I don't know."

"It's black. On your *face.* You want a *Black* face?"

Drawing the stool to the sink, Jia hauled her daughter onto it. Turned the water on high, gush pounding into the basin before swirling round the drain. Echoes, heard and seen, from that night. The door unhinged. Thump of many footsteps. Masked and black. White teeth...

"Ma—"

Dark skin and eyes. Back flash. *Who there?*

"Shut up and help me scrub!"

Jia continued scrubbing, repeating to herself the last dictionary entries she'd read, including the ones she added after browsing one of Hua's ethnic studies books.

miscegenation |miˌsejəˈnāSHən, misəjə-|
noun

the interbreeding of people considered to be of different
racial types.
ORIGIN mid 19th cent.: formed irregularly from Latin
miscere "to mix" + *genus "race"* + -ation.

mulatto |m(y)o͞o‾ˈlätō, -ˈlatō| dated or offensive
noun (pl. mulattoes or mulattos)
a person of mixed white and Black ancestry, especially a
person with one white and one Black parent.
ORIGIN late 16th cent.: from Spanish *mulato*, from
Arabic *muwallad "person of mixed race."*

tragic mulatto |ˈtrajik m(y)o͞o‾ˈlätō, -ˈlatō|
noun phrase/motif
a stereotypical character first appearing in American
literature; this archetype is depressed or suicidal due to
failure to fit whiteness or Blackness; the tragic mulatto
becomes victim to society's bifurcated vision of race,
which leaves no space for someone neither entirely Black
nor white.
Related entries: quadroon, octoroon

quadroon |kwäˈdro͞on‾| dated or offensive
noun
a person who is one-quarter Black by descent.
ORIGIN early 18th cent. (earlier as *quarteron*): via
French from Spanish *cuarterón*, from *cuarto 'quarter,'*
from Latin *quartus*; later assimilated to words beginning
with quadri-.

octoroon |ˌäktəˈro͞on‾| dated or offensive
noun
a person who is one-eighth Black by descent.

ORIGIN mid 19th cent.: from octo- *"eight,"* on the pattern of *quadroon.*

hapa |ˈhäpə, ˈhapə| (also **Hapa**)
noun US
a person who is partially of Asian or Pacific Islander descent.
ORIGIN Hawaiian, literally *"half."*

quapa |kwäˈpə|
noun US
a person who is one-quarter Asian or Pacific Islander by descent.

With her dictionary mantra and the sounds of vigorous cleansing, Jia could pretend to miss Fay's cries. Cries like *tong,* it hurts. Like *bu yao,* don't want. *Bai tuo*—mercy.

"This world has no mercy. Be strong. Shut up!"

Finished, Jia dabbed the sweat from her hairline. Towel over her face, Fay sat on her haunches, hands clinging to the stool. Jia reached out, fingers skimming Fay's back. But her daughter jerked away, inadvertently pitching herself into the edge of a cabinet.

"I-I'm sorry. Fay-ah. Let me see? *Now.* Listen to me! I'm going to see whether you like it or—"

In a surprisingly fluid motion, Fay stood up and spun around. Hands pressed to the incriminating cheek, she flung the towel at Jia's feet.

"Move your hands so Ma can see. Fay—hands down!"

The stain, gone, but in its place…. regret dug its heels into Jia's belly. Petechiae. Red specks, no bigger than the marks made by a freshly sharpened pencil, marched across her daughter's whole cheek. A colony of red dots.

DEAR DREW

JIA

EXCUSE THIS ENGLISH; AT MY work I have no need to use it, specially no writing. I write now with dictionary help.

I received your every letter. Always did. Read them until I could close my eyes, hear your big voice in my head. So big it feels like it's solid, like clay. I love your letters, how you detail the earth of your life. Your son looks healthy. Your wife too.

Sorry for all my silence. After everything passed, (is the phrasing "come to pass"?), I keep stewing. Wondering in a cycle. What if. I looked this up in my dictionary. You call "hypothetical." Example, a hypothetical situation. We call *jia ru*. Many ways to interpret, translate. Some translate to "imaginary." Others to "virtual." Or "to imagine." I best like to imagine.

Past (passed?) walls of language and culture, we share a same heart. If timing unfolded different, our families be together as one. What we are but fish? Baited and jerked through life's lines. We jump into our nets. These nets, our promises. Promises made for ourselves, for others.

Promise, a funny word. A declaration to do something, or that something will be done. I do this and you receive it. Holding promise means holding potential. But potential can fail. Making promise means more.

Cheng nuo. Commitment. Commitment to a deal, to sacrifice. Driving force, where we imagine future. The push to work at potential. And make promises unbroken truth. So much in one net! And think, all those crossing fibers that tie together lines we walk, mistakes and loss. Do we sew these fibers alone, together, or do fate hands hold this power? How much crisscrossing, intersecting points? Life lines, more complicated. Everything tied together in most unexpected ways. I fall off my thought.

I write to promise. To try, meet your letters. As fates want it. As balance needs. Because I believe sayings of my people. *You yuan wu fen.* Destined to meet, but never fated together. Written into two strokes, but united by one brush.

P.S. Keep sending photos. I store them safe.

P.P.S. I send you my own. Of Fay and me. Fay and Hua. Faith alone. If your wife finds these, tell her truth. You know me once. I'm honorary auntie to little Will. No worry about my Chinese scribbling below. Just character doodling.

Hypothetical: if ever you meet Fay, I think you two would meet in the middle. In between the strokes, in space unseen.

Sincerely,
Home

WHAT YOU WANT

———

Hua

"Two sisters, two sisters," Hua began, waiting for Fay to think of the next line.

The girl took her time, unfazed by Phil pausing his dishwashing to glance over.

"One old and strong, one young and smart. Your turn, Uncle Phil."

Hua's husband rattled off his contribution in Mandarin. "Each went her own way."

"One to the east."

"One to the west."

"Too much space in between."

"Eons passed without shared words."

"Without shared thoughts, without shared hearts."

Phil washed off the last dish as he closed the ditty. "What a shame, what a shame."

Bounding off the couch, Fay began drying the dishes and putting them away.

"No need, *sheng nu*, you're a guest here."

"Your ma's far away at a conference. We won't tell on you if you practice some entitlement."

Hua raised an eyebrow at her husband. "Entitlement? Don't get her into trouble."

"She's a bright kid, not a parrot. Besides, she never asked to be born. *Ow*—that's my shin!"

"No worries, *Ayi*. I know *Shu shu* means well but isn't really trustworthy."

For a moment only the sounds of swinging cabinets and clinking dishes filled the condo.

"I'm *untrustworthy*?"

Fay skipped toward the guestroom. Opening the door, she called over her shoulder, "Relax; nothing personal. Ma says you can never one hundred percent trust men."

Phil laughed. "But you can trust women one hundred percent?"

"Nope, just more than men."

"Anyone you can trust all the way?" Hua asked, watching her niece bob about in the doorway.

"No, but you can trust yourself the most. Okay, time for bed!"

"What is it, half past eight?"

Fay shook her head. "8:35 p.m. Ma says it takes normal people fifteen minutes to fall asleep, but I take twenty. Why are you staring, is there a stain on my shirt? Please tell me where so I can treat it. Do you have any stained clothes? I can treat those, too—"

"No stains, I just think—"

"Ma knows why—there's too much air in my *qi*. That's why she gave me breathing exercises to do before sleeping. *Xie xie* for dinner! *Wan an*, goodnight."

When the door clicked shut, Hua and Phil momentarily stared at it in silence.

"Were you like *that* at age seven?" he asked.

Hua chuckled. "Far from it. And you, Mr. Asian American? Mr. ABC?"

"Hell no. Some of my favorite activities included insulting my teachers, cutting off the cat's hair, and refusing to eat anything green."

"Sounds like the average American boy to me."

"I tried my best," Phil said, leaving the couch.

Hua heard the tinkle of glasses.

"Want a glass? Red or white?"

"What's the oldest open bottle?"

"Why does it matter?"

"Everything has an expiration date."

"Even more reason to ask for exactly what you want."

Her eyes drifted back to the closed door of the guest room. "What's the sense in asking for what's impossible?"

"Sorry, could you repeat that? You can speak up some; I doubt you'll wake Fay."

"Phil, it's—just give me what you'll be having."

"But—"

"I'll be happy with whatever you choose."

A BEING UNFORMED

EVERY MINUTE SHE SPENT WITH her niece, Hua took a mental snapshot. She believed that watching Fay grow up required continual vigilance. To take a break from Phil, from their coupledom, Hua volunteered to babysit for Jia.

Her mental camera kept her sane. The best kind of distraction: productive. Hua needed to be useful even outside the lecture hall, outside faculty meetings and manuscripts and papers and office hours.

The panoramas of Fay eased Hua's simmering blood. So many individual frames. By day's end, Hua strung them together, flipped through them quickly to initiate animation. The many, ever-changing faces of Fay. Like transient opera masks.

Thinking Fay, tongue between teeth, wavy hair almost touching her homework.

Obliging Fay, homemade Chinese food offering in hand, on visits to her dad, whom they only called Nelson.

Practicing Fay, brow fixed, weight on her toes, working her body and dance ribbon or Chinese yo-yo.

Listening Fay, eyes lower than the elder addressing her, torso leaning forward.

Observing Fay, limbs and features open, senses pulling and shifting and absorbing and assessing.

Speaking Fay, weighing each word in the mouth of her mind before its release.

Playing Fay, energy pulsing out of her pores like invisible orbs, unreserved, undecided and uncertain but for the notion that this face must fade soon.

Resting Fay, overtaken by exhaustion, no longer a servant to dictates and shame.

Hua loved them all, saw versions of her selves in Fay's faces. She wanted to freeze each frame, preserve each untouched essence. A child: a being unformed. A ball of clay, molding and unmolding due to the prodding and massaging of innumerable hands, fingers, fingerprints. New and teeming with possibilities.

But such freedom of form never lasts. With each passing year, the impressions begin to imprint. The power of influences take control. Instances of unmolding decrease. Definition, of shape, of name, sets the form. Continues to set it, hold it in place, until each portion learns its place.

The faces of Fay became molded masks. Hua ached to watch others hasten their setting process. And then the frequency of mask-wearing changed. Like performance articles of a bygone age, certain faces were relegated to the trunk of the past. Playing and Resting Fay received no or limited stage time. A girl could no longer be a child. A teenager could no longer be just a girl. A young adult could no longer be just a teen.

Knowing and observing, living these realities alongside and through her niece filled Hua's emptiness in the worst ways. It filled her with more hurt and longing. For what could have, should have been.

WHEEL BALANCE

FAY

"BEFORE RIBBONS, I LEARNED HOW to dance with a Chinese yo-yo. The western version's a diabolo. If you've been to a Chinese parade or New Year celebration, you've seen them.

"The Chinese yo-yo, or *che ling*, is typically four inches in diameter. It's made of two equal disks; a long axle connects the halves. Between the halves, you hook a string that's tied to two sticks. Two distinct parts compose the toy. In sum: two disks, intervening axle; two sticks, intervening string.

"You spin and throw the yo-yo in the air, alternating between swinging the string up and down; pulling it taut, letting it relax. All while maintaining the spin. So playing is like juggling. Except harder.

"There are many ways to perform with it. Some tricks include tossing it behind your back, Loop and Hook, Cat's Cradle, Matrix Orbits. Lots of practice. I learned these, and then how to dance with it. First I performed in talent shows, then competitions. I began to win. I'd gotten good. People knew it, Mom knew it, and then…then I got a *datou*. Big head.

"I'd show off, take unnecessary risks. I needed no one. Thought myself a self-pollinating flower. That's how I began losing. First the competitions, and then my confidence. Mom used child support money to buy me private lessons.

"An old man, eyes half-eaten by milk, taught me. Half blind, but never used a cane. Just knew his place in the world. Patient as a mountain, and once a champion. 'The yo-yo must never be dropped. It's precious, requires honoring, cradling, catching. Think. You spin, you hold the whole world on these strings. Nature. Your ma, your ba, all the people and things dear to you. You must take care. Control your speed and balance.'

"Wisdom a seven-year-old girl can't immediately appreciate. By that time, I'd picked up eye-rolling from my classmates. But after a daily hour of this kind of lesson, his metaphor sunk in. I'd re-imagine the yo-yo as the world. And on that world lived my parents and relatives and teachers and friends.

"I overcorrected. Believed too much in the metaphor. Each time I tossed the yo-yo, my heart heaved into my throat. I imagined dropping it, imagined the apocalyptic cries if it fell. I became good again—better—but out of fear.

"Finally my dad promised to attend a competition. But when it started, I found his face nowhere. He never promised unless he could follow through. I successfully completed the compulsory section, figuring weekend traffic delayed him. He'd be there for the one important to me, the freestyle.

"They introduced me for the freestyle. I took my place and began. Smiling, I lifted my leg over my head, threw the yo-yo in the air. I'd catch it in a second. I had time. So I looked. The empty seat stared back. I forgot about time, about the world. It crashed to the ground.

"I recovered quickly and finished the routine. I think I even placed. But he never showed. He never showed, and that's because, on the way to cheer me on, the front wheel of his vintage Harley locked up. Because the brake line got caught between the fuel tank and frame, causing a buildup of fluid pressure, causing the front wheel to stop spinning.

"After the funeral, I never played with the world again. For years I blamed myself, first directly, in a child's way. I failed to catch the spinning world, and my failure froze Dad's front wheel. I never told my mom I felt this way. Chinese people believe in fate; I wanted to avoid her judgment.

"When enough time had passed, I realized that the first event hadn't caused the other. But I held onto my shame, harboring it until film school.

"Why film? An accident, at first. A missed email. The wrong classroom. Embarrassment can make you stay. But with the lights out, the screen down, the images moving? In the dark, you see anew. You seek new. *The Grace Lee Project* changed my lens.

"So I switched directions. Received my first task. An odd assignment: write a ten-minute documentary in which you interview an object you dislike. I reached under the bed for the box containing my childhood relics. And I interviewed that yo-yo. I cursed it; I apologized to it; I wept over it. I held it. My old world."

DEAR DREW

JIA

HUA AND PHIL FINALLY WENT to the doctors. Sad confirmation of my suspicions. She put so much thinking to education and career, no room in her body for anything but knowledge. I keep this to myself. I know she'd get angry, yelling about my unability to cast off *mi xin*, superstition. Lecture on diaspora emigration immigration, then big words like acculturation, assimilation, integration. *How many years in this country? You're capable of change. You just refuse to learn…*

The doctors leave out Heaven's Mandate. Nothing written in heavens. No, they say everything measurable, learnable, knowable. Hua showed me the reports. Pages of word communities complex twisting before tired eyes. Most too technical to find in any of my dictionaries. The best reading in the summary. They say this result, this ending, at one time preventable. Her TB gave "pelvic inflammatory disease." No symptoms and caught late. Then damage done, irreversible. Hua "lament the negligence of her youth." Cursed herself. I told Phil she shouldn't cry. We each eat bitter fruit of fate. But he's second-generation Asian American and think I'm crazy. No, I see the world spin from forces of many directions. I hold more complexity in my peasant hands.

In ways, science helps: Action requires reaction. Nothing creates nothing and something creates something. But at same time, other forces at work, forces we too small to understand. Elements and nature has no mercy. Much uncontrollable exists. In Chinese we call this many names, sometimes fate. We must bow to it. Respect is different from waiting for death. We try, we work, we hope for luck. First step to knowledge is to declare, "I know little. And in this ever-whirling world, I know nothing." Trust, believe this, and *qian yuan wei liao*—your fate is yet unfulfilled.

On to your last letter. Happy that Will and Harmony do good in school and that Brenda got better nurse job. Thanks for those stock tips. Making money for that college fund seems easy now. Regret can't write more I hear Fay on the stairwell.

P.S. Enclose is a story Fay wrote for school. "Empress Earth" in pinyin is *Tu Huang Hou*. The Chinese version won cash prize, $30. I put half to college fund, other half in piggy bank you given her.

THE BREATHING DOLL OF CLAY

By Faith Wu Goodson

EMPRESS EARTH HAD MANY CHILDREN. Every spring, when she walked across the Heavens, her seeds fell from the sky like drops of rain. She loved them all, but secretly favored her mortal girl-child, Unity, who loved everyone and everything with wholeness of heart. Every time she visited the humans, Empress Earth stayed in her daughter's village the longest.

On Unity's twelfth birthday, her mother bestowed on her a doll of clay.

"Thanks, Earth Mother, for your generosity. I will fully love her."

Kissing Unity's head, Empress Earth said, "This doll looks like an ordinary clay doll. Four limbs, one head. Two eyebrows and eyes. One nose and mouth. Do you agree?"

"Yes, Earth Mother. She cannot furrow or wiggle her brows. She cannot blink or wink. She cannot smell or sneeze. She cannot open her mouth. It's clear for all to see."

"Ah, but this is really a special doll. When you find love, you'll learn. A doll of clay need not stay that way."

This comment puzzled Unity, but her nature rejected conflicting feelings, so the confusion passed. Empress Earth returned to the Heavens, and Unity returned to village life.

A month after the New Year, after the villages rolled away red banners, after the sounds of rattling firecrackers had faded, Unity walked to the river. Chores needed doing. Water must be collected. Clothes and cloths must be washed. She enjoyed scrubbing, rubbing away the stains. To clean is to purify through force. Purity, its simplicity, made her smile.

Static, Unity's cousin, approached the bank. He stopped short, watching. Her open, symmetrical face, cheeks pink from exertion, made him see her with new eyes.

"Good afternoon, cousin Unity."

"And to you, cousin Static."

He nodded at her washing. "What neat work you do. Perhaps you can help my mother? Since elder sister married, household management weighs heavy on her head."

Unity soon found herself living in Static's house, attending to his mother's bidding. While the mother suffered from fatigue, Unity sewed, cooked, cleaned, and accounted for the family's finances. At day's end, she collapsed onto a straw mat, tucking the clay doll in the nook of her arm.

Without visits to the market with Static, and playtime with the clay doll, questions might have whispered across Unity's mind. But these respites negated the possibility of discord. Besides, she'd grown to love Static's company. No longer did they tease each other like children. They talked about the evenness of the path and the consistencies of the seasons. He confessed his love for her, and with his kiss a new feeling awakened within her.

That night, the Moon Lady smiled down on the servant's quarters. Unity lifted the doll over her chest. It stared blankly. She sat up. And then, white light illuminating them, Unity kissed the doll. Her doll. She hugged it, heart brimming with love. She loved its smooth limbs, loved the contrast of its dark clay against her light skin. Eyes hovering on the edge of sleep, Unity lay down, placing it next to her. This doll, hers to love. To own.

"No. Love's an exchange. Between friends, equal companions."

Unity felt breathing on her neck. She turned to the voice. Seeing its source, Unity scrambled off the straw mat.

Life size. Four limbs, one head. Two eyebrows and eyes. One nose and mouth. She could furrow or wiggle her brows. She could blink or wink. She could smell or sneeze. She could open her mouth.

"There's nothing to be afraid of. We're still friends. Yes, come here. See? Now we can love each other."

The next morning, Unity found the clay doll had returned to its previous form. What a strange dream, she thought, before embarking on errands. Still, she kept it to herself, even when Static paused during their marriage plans to question her trance.

That night, when the Moon Lady visited, the dream awoke. Unity realized the pattern. By day she devoted herself to Static and her soon-to-be mother-in-law. By night she devoted herself to the breathing clay doll.

A month of this double living changed Unity. Questions began to surface in her mind, ones that remained. Ones that demanded answers. She buried them as best as she could.

The wedding ceremony took place. The tea ceremony performed, Unity moved to Static's quarters.

As he lifted her red veil, granting her permission to see other colors, the Moon Lady visited.

The clay doll woke, blossoming to life between them. "What about me?"

Static jumped back. "Where'd that Black girl come from?"

"I'm Unity's companion, created by Empress Earth."

Anger radiated from Static, crackling in the air. He stormed out, returning with his mother.

"Scheming fox-girl! My son's your husband. What's this Blackie doing here?"

"She's my clay doll friend. She comes alive at night."

Mother-in-law lunged for the doll, who danced out of reach.

"Hand her to me! You cannot love her anymore. You cannot be faithful to my son with her."

"Why can't I love both?"

"The heart is small. You have no room to love both. Splitting your love only leads to darkness. Besides, she's only a doll. It's just the trick of moonlight."

Unity stood in the way. "Look here, she breathes!"

"Static, hold her down!"

Mother-in-law took a pillow to the breathing clay doll.

Unity invoked her mother's name, Empress Earth. Her mother exchanged moon for sun. The mortals blinked under its rays. The doll shrunk and stilled. Empress Earth came to collect her.

"Earth Mother, if I cannot love both, I can no longer be Unity."

"You are simultaneously Unity and Disunity. You're too much for humans. Come with me, daughter."

They ascended to the Heavens, where Unity became Dyad.

WAITING FOR IT

Fay

MAYBE IT'S EASY FOR PEOPLE who've never felt the shackles of alienation to say, Stop hiding. But when you've seen this united front of bigots bludgeon your mothers and fathers and sisters and brothers; when you've seen this front target, taunt, rape, and even murder your lovers and friends; when you see the news reports of forsaken children prostituting themselves for sustenance and shelter; when you find yourself so afraid of rejection you practice, memorize the lie, perfecting the process until you question the roiling within, and feel disgust for yourself rise to your throat like bile, and feel this revulsion mutate into self-loathing, and feel yourself repress what's different because they tell you it's wrong so it must be true; when you realize you've built a set of accepted answers to be normal, whatever that is; when you stop imagining what it'd be like to be real and true; when you find yourself judging others because they're living out what you're struggling to suffocate; when you lie awake at night remembering shock therapy and reeducation; when you think you've made up the in-between because you feel like the only one lost in the balance; when silence eats your voice until you forget you have one; when you crave connection so much you'll bury your tainted parts so you can pass as one of the crowd; when you give up on hoping because it only leads to disappointment and loss—

PREPOSITIONAL LAYERS

JIA

IN MY PRACTICE, I SEE all people types. All kinds. Tongues, shapes, bodies. All kinds of skins and textures.

What's skin? Most outer layer. Covering. The peel of a potato, the rind of an orange. The bark of a tree. The lid on a teapot.

They try to hold their pain. To treat with gel, oils, baths. With long medicine names, pills on pills on pills. Nothing soothes these pains. Because they cannot reach it. Pain, often written beneath the layers of tissue and muscle. Inside, where mystery and magic meets.

They come like stray dogs. Eyes without certainness. Shoulders up to their ears. They point to their sunk chests. "You speak English?" They wave their hands like wipers: "I speak no Asian." I smile. I say, You here for relaxing. For relieving tension. Knots. Pins. Needles. Aching, crawling, twisting under skin. All unseen, but felt to core. They nod when they know: I know their need. I know what they need.

Stretched out, without coats and clothes, they point to arms, legs, feet. They never understand. Using their you-look-like-you-speak-no-English voice, I explain. No use looking. I talk to them. I ask what hurts. I listen. I ask with these trained hands. These hands find pain like maggots find wounds. You feel this? How bout this? And this?

Where's your mother source? Where the troubles, pain comes from. I circle, I sketch the folds, the lands of muscle. Here? Lower? Higher? Want me press harder? Deeper? Feel it? Tell me when. Tell me when I reach it, show me where to knead. Show me where to enter the needle.

Your stress shows. In these screaming nerves, these tight, inflexible strings. Think ignoring means problem's gone? Oh no. Problems never need your approval or acknowledgment to exist. To grow. Better face, own them before they own you. Many layers of skin. But only one body. Respect and treat it. Or it will fight your neglect.

It forever comes down to points. Pressure points. Locate the points, focus on them. The eye of the bull must rest there. Meridian, I say. "Prime meridian, you mean?" I shake my head, pointing to the poster on the wall. To definition two. And to below it.

> **meridian** |məˈridēən|
> noun
> 2) (in acupuncture and Chinese medicine) each of a set
> of pathways in the body along which vital energy is said
> to flow. There are twelve such pathways associated with
> specific organs.

> **qi** |CHē| (also **chi** or **ki**)
> noun
> the circulating life force whose existence and properties
> are the basis of much Chinese philosophy and medicine.
> ORIGIN from Chinese (Mandarin dialect) *qi*, literally
> *"air, breath."*

I amend, as Hua likes saying in English, my previous state. It forever returns to *qi*. The cycle, life force, life energy. For harmony, for yin and yang, *qi* must be stable, even. Forces must be equal.

DEAR DREW

JIA

SIMPLE ANSWER TO YOUR QUESTION: no. I have no worry. You underestimate my skill to keeping secrets where they belong. What use, this unearthing of the past? Helps no one, can't change. No more talk of history. Time swings in one direction. People meet, lives cross, but these just points on winding paths. You can look back, no turn back. Why mourn?

And when past resurfaces, when earth layers overturn, you face forward. No use imagining possibilities. Can spin life away with hypothetical. Ground yourself. Build roots, deep, thick.

No use writing next week: I return to Taiwan. My father's funeral. I fly back with Hua on Eva Air. No need for sorry. I lost count of years spent unspoken. Pride on both sides, sure. Secrets, too. I regret nothing. This makes me think...through all, so focused on surviving, on money, on providing for better future, I forgot. Forgot to thank you. For your role in dance of fate.

That's why I never considered abort. I could used the money from Hua to do. I could done it in weeks before that ticket date came round. Sometimes, looking through photo albums, I imagine.

The other alternative. With free body, but heavy mind, stepping on that plane. Watching San Francisco stretch greater and greater away. That bridge, the city lights, specks. Leaving our brief friendship to die in rebuilt Stanford. Returning to the island, no longer my island. Too changed, possibility killed home. To return to so small, so shallow a life. Always remembering the big America. Hating Hua. Hating myself for choosing known, too afraid the question marks. Here I go, breaking my own rules. I'm sorry. So many scattered thought.

Stay healthy. Hug Will and Harmony.

MIRAGE OF THE CITY
IN SUMMER

FAY

WALKING IN THE CITY, THE city teeming with bodies, means touching. Means swinging arms and legs, hands brushing, feet kicking, shoulder to shoulder, hand to hand, thigh to thigh. Exhaling your breath, inhaling the breath of others, exchanging air and saliva in mouthless kisses. Stumbling past body bubbles, breasts grazing, sweat jumping from host to host like lice. Everyone knows there's no room for apologizing. No time, no quiet, no space.

Walking in the summer, in the city of straight buildings, means unified passing. Means pressing forward in tandem, wildebeest swirled among zebras. Migrating in the quest for greener pastures, migration born of instinct, desire, imagination. Wildebeest and zebras, horns or stripes, lead with heads and hips and hearts. Into the center of darkness, for no migration, no sought transformation, evolves as planned. Everyone sees the gaping dark, the razors of the crocodiles.

Everyone crosses the river, wet coats turning into weights. Hears the grind and snap; the popping of jaws is the ripping of bones from sockets. The people-prey say nothing. Heads still, eyes straight, they trudge through, lifting feet from mud, finding momentum in the moving hips of the ones ahead. Propelling onward, listen to the drive, there's nothing but the drive, the drive, the throb.

The pulse picks up when the eyes spot the other bank. Wildebeest and zebras, north, east, south, west, and all the directions in between slip under. Sucked into the maws of predators. No returning, no circling back, no feeling for the other. The herd's together but rejects in this togetherness because each pair of eyes trains on the other side.

See the other side, where hope and faith live. City of warmth and fruit and summer without drought. On the other side, reality's the dream. What you want's what you need. What you need's what you get. What you get's what you give.

No one reaches the other side. But some get close.

WHEN THE HALVES MEET

FAY

CUT TO:

INT. WEST VILLAGE, NEW YORK - FAY'S 90-SQ-FT APT - TWILIGHT

Fay moves from sitting on the BED to the WINDOW LEDGE, lending her profile to the camera. The window is inched open.

                    SUMMER (O.S.)
          When'd you stop speaking Mandarin?

                    FAY
          Second semester of freshman year.

                    SUMMER (O.S.)
          Before we met. Who were you rooming with?

                    FAY
          Shania. From Portland. We still talk.
          Occasionally, via email.

                    SUMMER (O.S.)
          Were you friends?

                    FAY
          Due to convenience and location. She
          respected me and I her. We shared some
          values and valued giving space.

                    SUMMER (O.S.)
          So by second semester, you'd gotten
          comfortable with each other.

                    FAY
          We had a system. We lived in the arts
          dorm, so I fit in the least. Always
          studying, learning to code and edit,
          reading scripts, watching films and
          documentaries.

                   SUMMER (O.S.)
Honing your craft.

                   FAY
Trying to build a sense of craft. Shania
knew that I liked being alone. As an
extrovert, she didn't understand it, but
as I said, she respected me.

                   SUMMER (O.S.)
What'd she do?

                   FAY
Sculptor. Worked with clay. She made that
fairy for me. A couple Christmases ago.

Mid-shot of CLAY FAIRY on middle shelf.

                   SUMMER (O.S.)
Talented. Love how it has bat wings. It
supposed to resemble you?

Close-up of FAIRY, then of FAY.

                   FAY
Maybe? But then she got the hair wrong.
I don't have my mother's hair. And even
when she wore it long, Ma never put pins
in it like that.

                   SUMMER (O.S.)
She worked in the arts studio?

Beat.

                   FAY
Or at her girlfriend's apartment. She
had one off campus.

                   SUMMER (O.S.)
She go there often?

                   FAY
Only starting second semester. Because the
girlfriend had transferred from PSU. They'd
been long distance before that. Came out
together, dating since high school.

                     SUMMER (O.S.)
But?

                     FAY
During spring midterms, the girlfriend
broke up with her. Said they'd grown apart.
And she'd met someone new. That
afternoon I found Shania on our floor, an
empty bottle of cheap wine between her
legs.

Fay looks out the window.

                     SUMMER (O.S.)
How drunk?

                     FAY
Drunk enough. I cleaned her up in the
girls' bathroom. Afterward we sat on
her bed and watched *Casablanca*. We fell
to talking. Rather, she rambled. I
listened. Then, like that scene in *When
Harry Met Sally*, she went from crying to
coming on to me.

                     SUMMER (O.S.)
What? You never told me—

Fay snaps head to Summer.

                     FAY
You broke the wall!

                     SUMMER (O.S.)
When did I talk to the audience?

                     FAY
The professional wall between
interviewer and interviewee. I'll need
to cut that.

Beat.

                     SUMMER (O.S.)
What happened next?

> FAY
>
> Ma walked in. We hadn't locked the door.
> I'd forgotten she wanted to drop off a
> "surprise treat."

Mid-shot of Fay picking hair off her LOUNGE PANTS.

> FAY
>
> She said nothing. A sharp intake of
> breath. Put the tray bearing spring
> rolls on the floor. Stared for thirty
> seconds at me. Eyes like I'd betrayed
> her, again.

> SUMMER (O.S.)
>
> Again?

> FAY
>
> How she always looked at me when
> I shamed her. Like I confirmed her
> suspicions. (Pauses) I need a break.
> Stop recording.

DISSOLVE TO:

INT. FAY'S 90-SQ-FT APT, KITCHEN - DUSK

Fay sits on a too-small stool, METAL BOWL between her
legs. She swirls something in the water. Close-up
reveals two halves of a POMEGRANATE.

> FAY
>
> After that, Ma stopped talking to me.
> When second semester ended, I stayed
> with her younger sister. My Aunt Hua and
> her husband, Uncle Phil.

> SUMMER (O.S.)
>
> That's when you went on Mandarin strike?

> FAY
>
> Yes. Didn't start out as intentional.
> Maybe on an unconscious level. But she
> ignored me for all of sophomore year.

> SUMMER (O.S.)
>
> Then she met me.

Close-up of Fay's HANDS, dissecting the pomegranate.
She dunks the halves in the water, loosening the
fruit's INNER SKIN.

> FAY
> She loved you. She only talked to me
> when necessary.

> SUMMER (O.S.)
> Always wondered why she spoke to you in
> Mandarin but you'd respond in English.

> FAY
> It turned into an unspoken game between
> us. Me, English only. Her, Mandarin
> only. Never acknowledging how that shift
> came about.

Fay peels back skin folds. The POMEGRANATE SEEDS
shine. She plucks, distributing the red hearts into a
COLLECTION BOWL.

> SUMMER (O.S.)
> So she's imperfect, but she loves you.
> She gave you this apartment.

Wide shot of ninety-square-foot living space.

> FAY
> The apartment she raised me in. Gift or
> curse? Both. Memory trap.

> SUMMER (O.S.)
> Shania…what happened with her? That
> night. You talk about it?

> FAY
> We jumped apart. She apologized. Said
> she'd been vulnerable. In the wrong
> place. I could be her type. Then the
> matter of convenience. We moved past it.

Close-up of collection bowl's CONTENTS: accumulation of
little hearts.

> SUMMER (O.S.)
> She make you question your sexuality?

                    FAY
          No.

Fay's hands, prune-like from the water, turn over
a pomegranate half. The water threatens to spill.
Close-up of shell: INNER SKIN is pockmarked, empty.

                    FAY
          I'd been questioning that for a while.

                              CUT TO BLACK.

THE SON RISES IN THE WEST

HUA

"WHY AM I HERE? I have no idea. Fine, because Phil suggested this. Said I've been different. Agitated/restless/distant. Not as docile and obliging as usual. More reclusive.

"Depressed? I think that's extreme. More like…tired. Overworked, I guess, in more ways than one. First World problems, of course. I'm grateful to have them. It's easy to remember the problems we used to have.

"I always try to be grateful. But I think ingratitude and desire for 'more' are part of the human condition. Yes, I make six figures. I've had tenure for some time. My students and colleagues respect me. My books sell well. I live a privileged, stable life in an amenity-filled western condo with a husband who worships me. I work with him in the same department at the university. I enjoy spending time with our niece, who stayed with us for a time. I exercise, recycle, submit my taxes, and donate to charity. I'm so perfect it's boring.

"But let me tell you something. I'm sure you won't be surprised. My perfection lives and dies on paper. Paper perfect. Everything I am—rather, everything everyone thinks I am—is due to my childhood.

"My father was a KMT (Kuomintang) general. When he fled China with the Nationalists, he brought his pride with him. Bullied his way into having what he wanted, no matter the cost to others. That's how he married my mother. He played a nasty part in the 228 Incident and thrived during the White Terror.

"According to rumor from the housemaids, my older sister had a twin brother. He died at birth, supposedly because the nurse delivered my sister first. This could explain why Father disliked Jia so much, or the maids could've spun the story.

"They say girls are like water. Easily spilt, and once spilt, unable to return. But Father harbored a specific distaste for Jia. He resented the mere sight of her. She looks more like him: sharp, proud features. A temper, an aggressive vitality like his, too. 'Inappropriate' for a girl. Then Mother gave birth to me and couldn't bear children any longer.

"I became the vaunted child. The youngest, prettiest, and smartest—that's what Father told everyone. I received the privileges of a son. A comprehensive western education. While Jia struggled to pass her yearly exams, private tutors provided me with unneeded assistance.

"Indulged and fêted. Treated like a doll with manly brains. It went to my head, and I had so much empathy to learn, but failed to venture beyond my compassionless environment. I took my cues from the adults. I treated my only sibling, my only sister, like we all treated the Taiwanese aboriginals. I experienced no brainwashing. I did everything of my own volition. When I saw signs of Jia suffering, I ignored them. I thought she had no capacity for suffering. Because we reserved humanity for humans.

"If you applied Mao's Three Worlds Theory to our family unit, I belonged to the first world. Brains and Father's favor were my superpowers. Mother alternated between the second and third worlds. Jia never left the third world—he made her our own exploited nation.

"And maybe nothing would've changed, if not for my curious nature. The night of my tenth Chinese New Year, I noticed Jia slip away from the servants' headquarters. By that point everyone was drunk and falling asleep. So I followed her.

"We walked for what felt like hours. I followed her into a wooded area. In the clearing stood a massive set of conjoined cypress trees. 'Stood' is the wrong verb. They seemed to leap up from the soil. Their roots intertwined, but their concave trunks leaned away from each other, like each had been punched in the stomach. They were also connected by a branch. Like studying clouds, if you looked at the pair long enough, it looked like they were in the middle of a dance. Or were holding hands.

"There's a story affixed to these trees. A Romeo and Juliet kind of story, except the brash lovers die together. They jump off a rock, and these two trees spring up from the resting place of their bodies. *Fu qi,* like man and wife. Poetic, I suppose.

"Anyway, Jia scaled one of these trees with the dexterity of a monkey. I'd never climbed a tree before. I'd never been left to my own devices. But I believed she couldn't do anything I couldn't do. And Jia knew this, which is why she didn't stop me.

"She watched me fight my way to the top of the opposing tree. When I finally arrived, she nodded, like I'd confirmed her suspicions. Then she shimmied down. At the base of the trees, she looked up at me, and waited. I realized my situation: stuck.

"For a few minutes we stayed that way. She looking up. I looking down. In silence, we waited for the other's decision.

"Pride is stubborn. It loves and believes only in itself. If Jia hadn't begun walking away, we might've stayed there until a search party found us. I called out to her. Older sister, I cried, please help me. I'm scared.

"Again, she nodded. She climbed up my tree, but when she'd almost reached me, she stopped. I motioned her closer. I held out my hand, but she didn't reciprocate. She just stared at me.

"And for the first time, I studied what she held in her eyes. I noticed the anger, the sorrow. But above all else, I read her overwhelming pain. I bowed my head. I cried my shame. I gurgled apologies.

"She joined me on my regrettable perch. We sat there, legs touching, sharing the silence. We watched the beginnings of dawn. How the old sun began to climb from the east, sister rays crowning its glory. Then Jia shifted me onto her back and climbed us down. That's the day we became true sisters. The day we became friends."

INVENTORY

ON THE FIRST OF EACH month, Hua attached a clean, notepad-size sheet of paper to the side of their sleek steel refrigerator. For at least twenty-eight days, a "No one fights like a JD" magnet pinned the sheet in place. During the list's early stages, solely Hua attended to the ancestors of the current sheet.

Between the two of them, lists suited Phil's nature more than Hua's. But marriage changes both parties. Especially the one more accustomed to adapting. Like a teabag eventually stains its mug, hues of Phil had seeped into Hua. They lived by lists. Physical and virtual notes. Before the advent of laptop-based stickies, Post-it notes rainbowed their work and home desks. Now their iPhones and laptops pinged reminders. Now virtual stickies were their desktop backgrounds.

During the early days of their marriage, Hua often opened the refrigerator to discover items that led to questions. How long ago did we open this soy milk? Who bought this kombucha? Do the droplets on these peaches indicate condensation or a sweaty decline? Where did *this* come from? We never finished that?

Phil's perennial "When in doubt, throw it out" response unsettled Hua. She still remembered how her mother would boil spoilt rice for their dogs. Unlike most Taiwanese, the Wu clan could've afforded to discard the old, the subpar, the excess. But they'd never done so. Of all the American-English words she'd learned, Hua found "waste" the most difficult to accept.

To deal, Hua instated a food-inventory sheet. Flush left, date of acquisition. Center, name or description of item. Right, date of expiration. Since its installment, Hua thought what they fed their wastebasket belonged there.

Later tonight, when Phil returned from dinner with his NYU Press editor, he'd toss leftovers into the refrigerator. If Hua reminded him at his convenience, he'd update the inventory sheet. During tired times, she updated it without saying anything. He often felt more tired than she.

With the close of the month upon them, the sheet had filled up. The difference between their handwriting made their respective efforts clear. Hua's handwriting apologized: small, fragile lettering, well-kerned. Phil's prosecuted: large, bold lettering, wide character spacing. Eighteen out of twenty lines apologized.

Did everything have a shelf life? Patience? Denial? What about one's sense of self? How often should self-inventory be taken? What would a list of Hua look like?

6/19/89	JD secured; bar examination passed
4/24/90	Birth of Fay to Jia, birth of Aunt/*Ayi* Hua
9/15/93	Award of tenure to Hua
8/8/95	Marriage of Hua to Phil, birth of Mrs. Ting, death of Miss Wu
95–Present	Professor Ting; Mrs. Ting; what others deemed an integrated model of Asian-immigrant success

Between the margins, behind the personal and professional CV, languished the pieces of her forgotten-denied-negated selves. Hua never needed to update her self-inventory. Every mental pore continually reminded her of what had long ago expired.

DEAR DREW

JIA

LEAVING FOR TAIWAN, I GAVE Fay my apartment keys. I have misfortunate news. When I returned, settled back, I inventory like usual. Everything on place—except my broken teapot.

My teapot with its broken-off mouth-spout I sewed a covering for, between yarn bundles and folds of saved wrapping paper and ribbons, among Christmas bows with no more stick, under blankets and spare dishtowels in the chest in the box under my bed.

Off with that teapot's lid and everything's there—except Nelson's picture of you and me at hospital. That one, where you smile at me and Fay. Before you leave and Nelson stays.

Maybe I make fuss over nothing. Too sensitive, too reacting...but I worry. I sleep bad of late. Wake up with strain in neck. Too much built tension. My *qi* feels out of whack. Everything out balance. Bad enough *I* paid for massage.

Tell me this is paranoid. I'm paranoia. Because I know what she thinks. If she found it. If somehow she figured right, searched you, now knows. All names she thinks me. Hypocrite. Turning black to white. I think she know not the saying for this, *hei bai dian dao*: invert black and white. *Dare you shun me for loving both sides, for sticking my chopsticks to your racist way.*

Impossible. She knows nothing. I must moved that picture elsewhere. She found nothing. She can't know me enough, how I think, to find hiding spot in first place. I waste your time. *Ben dan.* Stupid egg. I shred this letter.

THE FALLACY
OF RETURNING

Jia

return |rə'tərn|
verb
[no obj.] come or go back to a place or person
ORIGIN Middle English: the verb from Old French
returner, from Latin *re-* "back" + *tornare* "to turn"; the
noun via Anglo-Norman French.

In Taiwan there is more focus on you, you all, we, and us. Landing
at Taoyuan Airport means switching back to Chinese and Taiwanese.
Means trading "I" for collective. Your tongue settles back to fluent
nativity but your mind wanders.

The world's older than the experiences we have. Earth Mother has
unending knowledge and memory. Her layers of soil contain all lived
history. Time past, recorded, compressed, in all such dirt. We think,
because we walk on her, because she lies beneath our feet, we're above
her.

Is an earthquake her version of laughing?

Her layers feed on change. On the transitions from substance to
dust and back again. Everything is remembered through the layers.
Each layer holds a multitude of memories. What would it be like, the
ability to possess so much strata of knowledge?

Jia. Home, family. *Da jia*. Everyone, big family. Home is where
home is, wherever it goes. What happens to home when it turns back?

Return, the verb, is to lie. What a misleading definition. There's
no homecoming. What you come home to is a foreign place. Like
dogs, we sniff each other, searching for familiarity. For confirmation,
to identify. But when the particles that compose you, when the facts

that composed the place you called homeland endure the ebbs and flows of time...they mutate. And once you mutate, you can't undo.

What's this? Each of your memories cries. Unrecognizable. Taipei 101, ice cream vendors, subways, miniskirts combat boots crop tops and iPhones. The 7-Elevens and Pizza Huts and Dominoes and *Maidanglao*, which you learn is *reverse translation* for McDonald's.

Disorientation. No matter what you learned as North East South West. Your compass has cracked. By changing, you damaged its face. So its needle spins and spins and spins like a broken record. The orienting arrow knows nothing. There's too much to focus on.

What of your smooth sister? That cool, eternal flower? Nothing surprises her. Everything one big unfazement. You detect no shock, no panic at the overpowering sense of unfamiliarity.

When you meet Mother—this is a meeting, no reunion—you cast widened eyes over her. She is shriveled. She smells like an army of mothballs. With Father dead, she seems larger than you remember. But she's much smaller than you hoped.

Downsized. The pack of servants, gone. In this post-KMT age, the privileges of oppression have faded. One apartment. One live-in caretaker. One parent, hanging on.

At the temple, in the stomach-churning smoke of incense, everyone collects at the altar. The sight of so much white creates a blankness that sounds a pounding between your temples. *Bai bai*, bow one, two, one hundred times. *E mi tuo Fo*, merciful Buddha. You chant, you nod, you cry for a man you appreciated as much as childbirth. You cry to make up for the lack of hired mourners.

Though twenty-five years stand between you and pre-American Jia, you know every motion, every nuance of tribute. Incense burns, but this is *bao fo jiao*. The wailing and clasping of Buddha's feet means what you meant to the Wu clan. Little. For them, you're the overcooked clumps of rice that cling to the pot. You know; you scraped yourself off those sides. Saw the brownness of your underbelly. Felt how flaky and parched your substance became.

And yet. You now return from America the beautiful country. America the fair. In all eyes besides Hua's, your value has altered. No. For them, you now hold value. On the other side of the ocean that divides you from them, you built a life. You made a child—a girl, yes, but an American-All girl.

You delivered something the one time Hua couldn't. You live luxury. No such thing as a poor American. How all envy and resent you for your lucky fortune.

Yet there's still much to pity you for. So alone with no husband. Many years since his tragic death. All you do, work and save. With a daughter too busy and proud to visit, if only once. *Ai-yo, bu zu wei wai ren dao*—keep between us two—Jia Wu *hei bai bu fen.* Unable to tell black from white; no other explanation. How else you let a girl spoil?

Aftermath. After the payments, burial, distribution of what the General left behind...what to do with Mother? With her unmatched looks and age. Seventy years. If she stayed here, sitting on the wealth he squirreled, how long before vengeance and greed sought her out? If she returned with her daughters...if she *left*, would she survive?

Would it be better to suffer in a world known or unknown?

Late one night, toward the end of the non-return, you and Hua discuss. A verbal weighing of the scales. You hear Mother inch her way over, her walker scraping the grout dividing each tile.

Daughters, *huo pu sa.* Take me with you. I weigh next to nothing. No need for even this walker. I can wriggle onto a plane like a worm. Lead and I follow. You're American now, I understand. No sense appealing to filial piety. Do you have the heart to become living Buddhas? Let my bowed head replace my kowtow. These knees fail me. I know what waits at my next crossroad. Let me take it in peace—with you near my sides.

This profane reversal of tradition has stripped you and your sister of words. The two of you, like lion-dancer heads, nod and blink and move your mouths.

No worries about my learning English. I hear you can rely on Chinese in Chinatown. And I still remember my Japanese. During my youth many mistook me for Japanese. I can be what's needed of me.

You nod and blink. Hua stands, snapping into professor mode. She is a blur of plans and fingers and technology. Mother joins you on the couch. Its already-sagging middle deflates with a sigh, bringing your bodies closer together. Through her flower-ridden skirt, you feel her tree-branch legs. They're quivering.

PRIMA FACIE BARRIERS

FAY

Translated from Mandarin Chinese

Grandma Wu: Almost every night after Jia told me, I dreamed of meeting you.

Fay: Why?

Grandma Wu: Because you dream of the improbable. Did your mother ever play Teresa Teng for you?

("Sweet as Honey" instrumental clip)
(Clip fades)

Fay: She only played language tapes.

Grandma Wu: I always loved "Sweet as Honey" more than "The Moon Represents My Heart." The title's misleadingly simple. The song compares the loved one's smile to honey and spring flowers. But it's really about knowing someone through dreams. For twenty-five years, that's what you've been to me. The scent of spring in my dreams.

Fay: Um. Thanks. I thought of meeting you too.

(A beat.)

Grandma Wu: What did your mother tell you about me?

Fay: Not much.

Grandma Wu: She still resents me.

Fay: No, I'm sure she—

Grandma Wu: Come, granddaughter, your aunt told me you're a filmmaker.

Fay: Documentarian. It's more of a hobby—

Grandma Wu: Label it as such and it'll remain that way. As a filmmaker, surely you know much runs alongside and beneath what's spoken. Now we speak in specifics, in Chinese. But most body language needs no translation. My eyes have become weak, but my vision's the strongest it's ever been.

Fay: How'd I give myself away?

Grandma Wu: You've been rolling your lips like swallowing your mouth will save you.

Fay: You surprise me. Ma always said a wallflower had more backbone than you.

Grandma Wu: (Laughing) Creative of her. Between you and me, your mom's stronger than me and your aunt. A survivor in the truest sense of the word. Hua and I live on what others ask of us. We asked nothing... thought almost nothing, of your mother. Under her circumstances, everyone expected her to grow into a dull flame. Feel her now—quite a hungry fire.

THE NIGHTMARE RECURS

JIA

hypnopompic |ˌhipnəˈpämpik|
adjective Psychology
of or relating to the state immediately preceding waking
up.
ORIGIN early 20th cent.: from Greek *hupnos* "sleep" +
pompē "sending away."

EVERY TIME, THIS HYPNOPOMPIC OVERLASTS its welcome. Like a flea
eating dog, it lingers even after leaving.

I know the nightmare in the dark and in the day. Shadows or light.
Cold or warm. I feel the same skin-twitching chill. It's that night. That
night in question.

In a version of that apartment. Smell of excretions. And bubbled
sweat. Metal taste of blood-bloomed tongue.

It begins with the shattering. Then the unlocking, unfamiliar from
this side, in that direction. Wake, awake, waken! Pounding of pulse
match pounding of footstep sets.

Rustling of night-made cloth. No amount of ancestor worshipping
can save me from the coming. Clutch unborn Fay, faithful enveloped
watcher. I hear her heart in my stomach, mine frantic above.

Later, this date haunts that American tradition. This event is that
hallow of horror.

In this repeat mind show, Fay unlocks my button, unzips my belly.
Placenta bursts and I feel it burn like sun poison. She leaves, umbilical
cord round a spindle neck, cord end trailing like dragon's tail.

Those thick voices close. I open this dummy mouth to puppet my
salvation. But my self leaves, too. No soul, no center, no *qi*. No breath
for sound.

The leader sings. Alternated to reality. A superimposing.

Fishy chink, fishy chink!

Their thoughts, I hear them. Smell so fresh. On this boat we rock together.

Gut a fish in fear. It tastes stronger raw or cooked. Because you patted its cheeks with your knife. Drew a smile with metal teeth. Plucked its scales by use of your dirt-dug crescent nails. Glint of metal and bone pearls.

I had dreams...

I am gutted. Toss me. First, in the closet. Then, in a well. Deep down, like the ends of a root. Root finger pointing south. A wall encircling me. Paved. Nothing to grip onto. No cracks, no grooves, no indents.

But still I paw. And look up, up, up, up. Shadow and black night swirling. Stomach balloon burst. Faith hole. Craning my neck for a spot of clearness, clarity.

The hole, the opening, four by four feet. *Si* by *si*. Death by fours, death by death.

Crane, fishy chink, crane.

Nostrils flood with smoke. I open my dummy mouth to gulp wet air. Nothing, nothing to drink. I gasp without noise or function.

Hypnopompic thrash. Claw beneath surface. Bubbles rise to the top to break.

I know it can repeat again. Nightmare revisited.

But I wake, looking up, up, up, up. My neck always hurts.

A TAIWANESE ARGUMENT

Jia: What?

Mother Wu: You dare to use that tone with me?

Jia: Stop being dramatic. You're the one who's staring critically.

Mother Wu: You've always been paranoid.

Jia: You're the one with a never-ending hidden agenda.

Mother Wu: If I didn't have arthritis, I'd remind you of your place.

Jia: Careful, Ma. Remember where you are. In this country, I owe you nothing.

Mother Wu: That's what this is about, ah? Those pamphlets. Hua doesn't have the discipline to consider maintaining me. But you—you know better. Think you can ship me to some factory for old people? Where strangers will help hasten my death?

Jia: I believe in karma.

Mother Wu: You believe in vengeance.

Jia: We get what we give.

Mother Wu: You don't get to choose. These rules exist for a reason. You can't rewrite the cycle of family.

Jia: Stop trying to justify the arbitrary nature of Confucianism.

Mother Wu: What's this really about? Your father?

Jia: He's dead. I don't waste my time on the dead.

Mother Wu: Where's your face? Who raised you?

Jia: Not even the nanny. You lost me in more ways than one during the Ghost Festival.

Mother Wu: Which one? Which part of the festival?

Jia:	Your missing memory speaks volumes. The thirteenth day of my second lantern procession.
Mother Wu:	Impossible. What a storyteller. No two-year-old child is capable of holding memories.
Jia:	According to you, perhaps.
Mother Wu:	Lower your voice! I'm sure the neighbors are sick of your shouting.
Jia:	This is *my* apartment. You're my imposing guest. And why does it matter? None of them are Taiwanese. We're just spouting gibberish to them!
Mother Wu:	Hua would never lower our family this way.
Jia:	I tripped. You neglected me and stomped on me while you turned away. I'm lucky no strange man nabbed me!
Mother Wu:	What do you know about being kidnapped? Being held against your will? Becoming one man's willing slave? You stinking coward.
Jia:	I fought for little triumphs. *You* took the fox way out. I dug my own path. What visible scars do you possess? Foolish old woman. You're the sheltered one!
Mother Wu:	You think you can compete with my experiences? Go cry from hunger.
Jia:	You never experienced true hunger. The kind that first twists your stomach, but then relaxes. The kind that hisses, but then curls inside your stomach for an indefinite rest. Bitch about your KMT-wife troubles all you want—you don't know the feeling of absence. Of buried emptiness.
Mother Wu:	You talk like a turtle egg. Presumptuous! Get out before you give me a stroke.
Jia:	With pleasure! Enjoy my empty apartment.

THIS SO-CALLED
LIBERAL TOWN

Fay

I‍f my eyes were a camera, this is the short I'd shoot. My subway-ride moving picture. A monologue dramatic fit for stage but interpreted from my filmic pupils. Dilate. Action. Action through words.

CUT TO:

INT. SOUTHBOUND 1 TRAIN, NEW YORK - SUBWAY CAR - DUSK

SITTING MAN holding *THE NEW YORK TIMES* spreads legs
as the 1 screeches to a halt. Window that should show
the station's mosaic is obscured by the bulk of bodies
wearing jackets. In the cracks between jackets peek
slivers of the bold Marble Hill sign. People struggle
off and on. Voices of passengers continually overlap.

                    PASSENGER 1 (O.S.)
          No, I'm on my way to Whole Foods now.

                    PASSENGER 2 (O.S.)
          Just got out of class.

                    PASSENGER 3 (O.S.)
          Where you at?

                    PASSENGER 4 (O.S.)
          Not a good time.

                    PASSENGER 5 (O.S.)
          'Course I didn't get off work.

Train jerks back into motion. Sitting man snaps
NEWSPAPER PAGES back and forth. The pages cover his
face. He reaches the last page and begins the snapping
process again. The snaps are louder. A page tears. Two
passengers look over briefly before returning to their
phones. Sitting man folds the paper and looks for eye
contact. No one notices him or his throat. His Adam's

apple lurches. It's like a frog about to leap out of
his mouth.

Train passes through a tunnel. In the dark, sitting
man's voice knifes through the voices. His voice is
smooth and assertive, younger sounding than he looks.

> SITTING MAN (O.S.)
> Not one mention. In this whole reputedly
> prestigious broadsheet, not one mention.

Train emerges from tunnel. City lights briefly filter
through the car before it plunges underground. The
dim underground lights only illuminate passengers'
silhouettes.

> SITTING MAN
> Brother, let me tell you something.
> This so-called liberal town is replete
> with corruption. No one's thinking.
> Everyone's either a drone or a
> corruptor.

> PASSENGER 1 (O.S.)
> Do you mind?

> SITTING MAN
> Not one mention. It's the bankers.
> They own this town. Got the whole damn
> country in their pockets. Liberal media,
> politicians, universities. All comes
> down to corporate interests. Capitalism,
> death to man.

> CONDUCTOR via INTERCOM (O.S.)
> Ninety-Sixth Street. Transfer here to 2
> or 3. Eighty-Sixth next.

Some passengers look from sitting man to the clear
night before following others off.

> SITTING MAN
> Not one mention. Don't get me wrong.
> It's still a race war. We still live in
> a world dependent upon the simplicity
> of appearance. Even Obama's sipped the

binary Kool-Aid. Says he's just a Black
man.

               PASSENGER 2 (O.S.)
No, it's just some nut job.

               CONDUCTOR via INTERCOM (O.S.)
Eighty-Sixth Street. Seventy-Ninth next.

               SITTING MAN
Not one mention. The world, but this
country especially, refuses to acknowledge
us. My fair skin *and* afro. All in the
features, they say. Eponymous: featuring
your features. Your broad nose. They
mentally measure it.

               CONDUCTOR via INTERCOM (O.S.)
Seventy-Ninth Street. Seventy-Second next.

               SITTING MAN
Hypodescent. The stakeholders codify a
national racial conspiracy. Everybody's
trying to pass. Only time Black's good
is when you're *in* the black. Black is
beautiful, but also, *being* Black in this
country? It's work.

               PASSENGER 3 (O.S.)
He's just upset *he* can't play with the
big boys on Wall Street.

               CONDUCTOR via INTERCOM (O.S.)
Seventy-Second Street. Sixty-Sixth,
Lincoln Center next.

               SITTING MAN
Not one mention. No one really makes
it. I know, what about Beyoncé? Nicki?
Oprah? Denzel and Samuel? Black
exceptionalism. Or sellouts. Pretending
they aren't like us. And guess what?
The net worth of all of them *combined*
doesn't begin to touch that of all the
fat-cat investment bankers, hedge fund
managers, psychopathic CEOs. You know
what a psychopath is? People misconstrue

the term. Psychopaths are devoid of
feeling. Got no empathy. Treat us like
objects because their psychopathic
slave-owning ancestors indoctrinated
them in Manifest Destiny.

                    PASSENGER 4 (O.S.)
Yeah, welcome to the NYC subway, lady. A
moving soapbox.

                    CONDUCTOR via INTERCOM (O.S.)
Sixty-Sixth Street. Fifty-Ninth,
Columbus Circle next.

                    SITTING MAN
Not one mention. Yet their descendants
worship our athletes. Say that's the
place to relegate us. Besides prisons.
Sports: the new slave frontier. But
it's not slavery if it's consensual? If
there's endorsement deals and fame and
airtime and cars and women. The five-
star treatment. Sell your skin and brawn
like colonial times. Reappropriated,
repurposed, but the heart of the
matter's the same. And those worshipping
white boys? They don't know *history*.
Catch the ball and run faster, 'cause
that's all *you people* know how to do
good. Just mules tossing around a ball.
Nothing up there to concuss. Every Black
body still subject to the terms and
conditions of hoary men.

                    PASSENGER 5 (O.S.)
Where do you get off, man?

                    CONDUCTOR via INTERCOM (O.S.)
Fifty-Ninth, Columbus Circle. Fiftieth
next.

                    SITTING MAN
Not one mention in this whole goddamn
supposedly liberal magazine about Martin
Luther King Junior Day. Not one fucking
lily-lipped mention. Okay, go ahead,

lamb-of-God sheep. Walk off this rickety
train and step out onto ground the
white man consecrated because fucking
pompous ignorant Columbus found the
wrong America and couldn't own up to
his mistake. You want to talk history?
In a nutshell, brother. The white man
uproots, enslaves, and fucks over
the natives. And then devotes school
activities to Columbus idols that piss
on the face of Dr. MLK. I ask you, what
kind of country do we live in? What is
this town? Where is the humanity, or
have the psychopaths brainwashed and
eaten it all because everything's a
fucking power struggle and Hobbesian and
fucked, fucked, fucked!

NO LINES
TO READ BETWEEN

HUA GLANCED UP FROM "BEYOND the Privacy Principle" to find Phil's hand on her knee. She returned her gaze to Kendall Thomas's article, but the hand remained. Hua flipped to the next page, found a riveting paragraph, and highlighted vigorously. The hand remained. She underlined. Pushed up her glasses to read a footnote. Wrote what she meant to be a short note that meandered onto an additional page. No need to look. All in the feeling, the clammy heat. Still the hand. It moved. She turned another page and the action sounded like scraping.

He cleared his throat. "Now a bad time?"

"For what?"

"For a break."

"You're right; it's past time I went to the bathroom."

On the toilet, Hua listened to herself tinkle. She sat, staring at the peach-colored tiles, until she tricked her body into dripping again. Rising, she took care to wipe the space between. The space she tried to ignore, to the point of erasure.

Stepping to the sink, she turned on the faucet. Under the cover of ablution, she whispered the one-syllable word. Once. Twice. Wiped the sweat off her forehead and pulled the door toward her. Stepped over the threshold.

"Everything okay?"

Hua picked up the article and her pencil but stayed standing. She held the article in front of her chest, the perfect paper shield. "I haven't reread this article in five years. It's engrossing."

Phil nodded at her side of the bed, her lower body's previous occupation evident in a wrinkled imprint. "Come on, when did you forget how to turn off?"

Like a girl finally able to show and tell, Hua held the article higher. "I'm brushing up for tomorrow morning."

"As if you need to."

"You can never be overprepared."

"I respectfully disagree." Phil patted the imprint.

Hua swallowed her accumulated saliva. Stared at the evidence of her lower body's existence, its traitorous physicality.

"You look like you need a massage. Desperately."

"I don't mean to."

Phil chuckled. "I doubt anyone means to look stressed."

"I suppose desperation has never been in vogue."

He smiled in that particular way. The way a man smiles when he's sure of the eventual outcome.

"Think you can massage me to sleep?"

"Relax those papers and I can do more than that."

Hua placed the article on the nightstand, rested the pencil atop it. So many words in her head, in reach of her hands. But only one best conveyed her feeling. A most obvious, a most hurtful word.

She resumed her position, aligning body to imprint until she'd covered the wrinkles with her presence.

Before he could draw closer, Hua pulled the covers over her length, yawning. "Seems like my body's taking away your job."

"But it's only eight!"

"Maybe I'll get up at four tomorrow."

"To do what?"

"Jog around Central Park."

"It'll be dark."

"I own a flashlight."

Phil sighed. "What's this really about?"

Hua blinked rapidly. "Nothing. I'm just tired."

"Dr. Morass isn't helping."

"I'm not depressed."

"It's nothing to be ashamed of. We all have needs."

"I know, Phil. No need to remind me. I'm no *child*."

He winced. "I meant—"

"I know. I'm sorry. I'm sure we're both sorry."

Minutes passed while they lay under the weight of the silence.

"If you want—"

"I wanted to try—"

Hua patted her husband's knee. She withdrew her hand but his own captured hers. The one-syllable word lingered on her tongue. Swallowing, she chased it with her rancor.

FALLEN HAIR

HUA

"GOOD TO SEE YOU AS well, Dr. Morass. Oh, just the usual kind of busy. Lectures, grading, office hours, conferences, speaking engagements.

"I think you should change that questionnaire. Seems to me that it's skewed. Zero to five, sure, a fine graduated scale. But the phrases you pair with the numbers are too general. The questionnaire leaves no room for the in between.

"We possess plenty of in-between feelings, sentiments of all kinds and scopes. The depth of human emotion never fails to surprise me. Once the base of Maslow's needs is fulfilled, we want to hold that elusive sense of self, to actualize it. Watch it stand before us, perform a twirl.

"Zero, 'none at all.' I suppose that could stand as is. But one, 'several times per week'? Two, 'almost every day'? Three, 'every day'? Four, 'several times per day'? Five, I suppose, is inevitable. Though 'all the time' also seems excessive. Why not allow for a more open-ended questionnaire? When you ask people to check little boxes or circle generic phrases, aren't results tainted? Don't you lead participants to select certain answers, or leave them no choice but to settle for what can't suit them?

"I'm not upset. I'm merely inquiring to understand the mechanisms behind the machinery. Of course, I understand the nuances of the psyche. Yes, I used an ill-suited analogy. But that's my point regarding your questionnaire. No wonder you have to hand everyone the additional questionnaire. The questions pressure everyone to feel depressed or vulnerable!

"I *am* calm. I admit I feel stressed. But in a controlled way: I'm handling and managing as I always do. Obsessed with perfection? Hardly. I know the quest for perfection is an ill-fated one. Am I happy?

Why? What right does one have to happiness? The constitution merely grants the *pursuit* of happiness. The state of happiness is individualistic and therefore incapable of being guaranteed. American happiness is pleasure-seeking, and it's an endless chase. But Buddhist nirvana's too lofty for me. What am I left with?

"I'm only defending and thinking of all possibilities. Too many doctors have seen me. It's been a revolving door of appointments.

"Perhaps I'll cut my hair. The last time I wore it short was in undergrad. I could donate ten inches and still have enough to play with. I like the imagined feeling of that. Cutting the dead weight off. Hair is dead. Release it unto its next incarnation."

DEAR DREW

JIA

I ATE YOUR LAST LETTER. In figurate sense, with mouth of my mind. Will and Harmony are dream children. I wish…do we really know what we wish? Can we?

Massaging and managing other *qi* gives me endless time to thinking. I say all those right words to maintain good relationship with clients. But my mouth becomes automatic. Move up? Deeper? Resist my fingers. Lean into my hands. Become dough. Elastic, give, push, pull.

Thinking during the work. Passively active body, but full active mind. Wishing. To wish means to hope, to imagine alternate to current reality. Like how Fay told me, a computer produces so many algorithms. Our minds create these alternate. These imagined answers to "if" statements. Depend on time and circumstantial.

If lists. I think them during sessions. Digging my knuckles into a man's hairy white back, I thought list.

If.

I born first. The wanted, vaunted one. Brainy beauty. Adored in two countries, by relatives and friends. Offered security of respected suitors.

Able to choose or avoid offspring. That funny word and reality. A child, being that springs from off your genes, from out your body. The choice of physical and childless freedom.

Able to leave family behind, drop them like the cracked dishes they be.

Could find and develop interests. Instead of scrabbling for any job, holding change in hands sweat sticky, living in temporaries that always become permanents.

If only life offered blueprints for revise. Simple erasing, shifting, re-sketching.

What a dream, this. Dream of ease and peace. If you unhappy in mind, you unhappy in existence. Your body can function without mind's approval. But you can't tell yourself to feel other.

I feel…too much. I think we all do. You know I feel greatest vulnerable with you. I still see you in my eyes of mind. How you helped me. Accepted me, linked me to Nelson, to work that leaves me time to think.

Si xue. Vulnerable. Vulnerable-sounding word, too. But I feel no fear of attack when I think of you. I know you know me, unlike anyone, even Fay. But still, no fear. I call your face, your voice, through your words, and feel right in my uncertainties.

I hope you and Brenda together work out everything. You forever are my true and one friend.

RED-CARPET TONGUE

peel 1 |pēl|
 verb
 1 [*with obj.*] remove the outer covering or skin
 ORIGIN Middle English (in the sense "to plunder"):
 variant of dialect *pill*, from Latin *pilare* "to strip hair
 from," from *pilus* "hair." The differentiation of *peel* and
 pill may have been by association with the French verbs
 peler "to peel" and *piller* "to pillage."

ISN'T IT FUNNY, THE WAY I peel me apart? Forgive foreign alien tongue.
I own this faulty mouth, this faulty speaking contraption. Trained into
silence. After splitting these lips with poison of tongue's tip, I locked
my jaw.

What's a mouth? A hole. Look into the holes of a drain. The dark
mouths. Where do they lead? What events do mouth portend? This
tongue trips. This white language I learned rolls in my tongue, wayward
tiger mama.

If I peel the flecks of skin, the split strips of deadness leeching these
dried lips, what then? If I pillage myself, lick my wounds fresh, what
then?

Would all my debt be paid? Would the ancestors and ghosts bury
themselves in promised dust? Would crying Jia finally sleep?

Long gone are days of rouge lips, flat layers of plums for spilling
sweetness.

I roll this tongue out to examine these white flecks. To see where
the tastes bud and die. Nothing lasts, especially not happy memories.
They pass through like unfilling, almost-grasped meals. Like immigrant
mother's efforts for rebel whitewash child.

LONGING
FOR DOORS

Fay:	Do you think I should leave this apartment?
Summer:	Because you grew up here?
Fay:	Maybe. How many memories can one place hold? And because I have no doors. This is just one open box. I'm a hamster in a tank.
Summer:	But your rent is absurdly low. You can walk to work. And the bodega on the corner sells wholesome bananas.
Fay:	But I dream of doors. Of the possibility of opening and closing them at will.
Summer:	I think you just want to compartmentalize.
Fay:	What's wrong with that? I want a fucking closet. To use it to shove in all the crap I don't care about or have time to deal with. Stow away until I'm capable of cleaning. Look at all these rods, at all this open space. All my clothes and jackets and shoes out for view like I'm living in a display case.
Summer:	People rarely clean out their closets. You think hiding will help? Out of sight...
Fay:	I know what's in my mind. I keep mental stock. It's a labyrinth up here. Head case.
Summer:	Sometimes I wonder if you enjoy self-flagellation.
Fay:	Do you think we're a love story that will never happen?
Summer:	Do I think what? We're what?
Fay:	Nothing. Just some lyrics from a song.
Summer:	Have I heard it before?
Fay:	No. It didn't go the distance.

Summer: Do you think we torture ourselves because we can't find the right doors?

Fay: I think we peripherally know where the right doors are. Seeking them out is too frightening. Much more comfortable to bang on the wrong doors. The ones we can never be admitted to. To try and pick the welded locks. Less productive, but achingly familiar.

Summer: Continuity isn't questionable.

Fay: If it's unbroken...

Summer: Then it's inherently unfixable.

Fay: The hinged door. The soundless wheel.

Summer: I don't want to influence you, but I'd stay here.

Fay: Doorless?

Summer: Without doors, you've got one large portal. Nothing preventing you from rearranging. No borders, change in terrain from tile to carpet, no frames or walls to limit your height.

Fay: I want to open and close at will. To cordon myself. Shut out and off.

Summer: Light switches for your mind?

Fay: I want the bliss of darkness. The lights Ma left me are blinding. So Taiwanese, like a FOB restaurant. I see every flaw, every crack in the wall.

Summer: You'd rather sleep with spiders?

Fay: I want to live alongside the neglected.

Summer: Without interacting.

Fay: With barriers. Doors between us.

EVOLUTIONARILY
SPEAKING

FAY

"NELSON. GOODSON. SON OF NEL? Son of Good? Are we meant to become our names? Or to reject them? Or to juggle the balance?

"My father inherited paternal legacies. Like a lassoed mustang, my father strained against rope fibers. Teethed at their burns. He hated the office life. Longed for the rush of the drive, the shrieking whip of wind, the strain of self-imposed weight. People like that spend every uncaged moment attempting to exterminate all seconds of suffocation. Risk is their only reward.

"In my memory vault, I hold an illicit treasure. A five-year-old girl's stolen moment. I play it like a favorite record. So lovingly abused, some grooves have smoothed. My needle hesitates and skips. But the essence of the song transmits.

"I never called him 'Dad.' Nor 'Daddy,' 'Father,' 'Pop,' 'Papa,' and certainly never 'Ba.' 'Just Nelson,' he said, and Ma agreed. I thought I'd sprung from his forehead like Athena from Zeus. Related in an intimately distant kind of way.

"When too many clients booked Ma, she worked overtime. She always tried to pass me on to my aunt and her husband. But, as distinguished professors, they sometimes traveled for conferences. I loved when all schedules misaligned—this left Ma no choice but to leave me with Nelson.

"Upon deeper reflection, this memory might be corrupted. For what five-year-old girl belongs on the back of a motorcycle, even if properly strapped and protected? What father, untamed or tamed, would take his youngling on so wild a ride?

"Admittedly, Nelson rode slowly. But twenty-five miles per hour is a roller coaster for a child still capable of remembering the struggle to crawl. A sensational springtime experience. Blurred uniform brownstones and traffic lights. Smell of vendor peanuts and street grime and car exhaust. Tunnel out. Away. Onto road like an unrolled gray tongue, outstretched and lazy. Hair strands in a mouth salivating with excitement. Squeal eaten by the compressed air. Rev of steel-horse motor. Little-girl hands, sweaty and slipping, fumbling with the back of a cracked, musty leather jacket. Eyes tearing: dust or feeling or both. Love lost to the escape of speed.

"But I remember the B-side, too. The return to zero. Killed ignition. Tunnel birthing us back into chaos. Back to the boxed life; to the wailing walls of paper; the clogged, shared bathroom—smelling, smearing of human releases; the clumps of non-familial, unfamiliar hair suffocating shower drains. To the Sit Still while I Rip Through Your Hair with these Metal Teeth life. Ghost of a forehead kiss and the pass off and the slamming door. The endless sound of Ma locking me in.

"This is how you love me. Through many acts of leaving me. It's not forbidden fruit if no one says it's always out of reach.

"I've heard that the firstborn child is supposed to most resemble the father. Nature's visual attempt to convince the father to stay. Nature's silent reminder. Look at me. At how this face mirrors yours. I am your progeny. Continue to claim this blood, these features, these genes, this skin shade. Part for whole. Your synecdoche. Maybe that's why he always left. My Asian face purrs Ma, Ma, Ma. Visual alienation."

DREAM OF THE VOID

HUA

"MY LATEST DREAM? IT'S ONE out of two that recur. This and dreams of my teeth falling out.

"The dream arrives in the middle of the night, usually at three in the morning. Whatever scenario I'm imagining shifts in this new direction. I know it's impending because I feel the urgency rise. Pressure builds inside like a shaken glass bottle of soda. I feel my innards bubbling.

"All I can think is 'I need, I need,' over and over again. But I can't finish the thought. It's like a word tripping on the folds of one's tongue. I feel and *know* the name, but the…entity evades my attempts to reveal it.

"And then the need appears, bursts from the depths of my ocean mind. No matter if its functionality is impossible. It surfaces and stays, waiting for my use.

"I see and recognize. But my feet are anvils. And, concurrently, still the pressure. I know I need relief. That my reliever waits, available, a mere two steps away. But I stay, rocking side to side.

"Finally, my eyes tear. The pressure's traveled too far north. Suddenly the anvils disappear. I shuffle forward like my feet are bound. My knees reach it first. If I'd been wearing pants, I'm now wearing a skirt or dress. Without stockings or tights. The porcelain's cool against my kneecaps.

"I turn around and it's a yearlong rotation. I'm excited at the result waiting on the other side. But there's a warning buzz in the eye of my mind. No, if I meant 'ear,' I'd have said so. Please, it's *my* dream. Sorry, just let me finish.

"Now, knee backs to the porcelain, I sweep up my skirt or dress, holding its hem under my chin like I did while a girl. The underside of the fabric and its seams scratch my upper neck.

"Yes, sometimes people watch me. I never know them. Men and women. All races except my own. More women? I never remember that. They stand around, waiting, and sometimes stare without meeting my eyes. In my most recent dream, I'd been at the beach. Everyone but me wearing only swimsuit bottoms. I'm in a flowery, A-line sundress.

"Anyway, chin cradling my dress bottom like one cradles a phone, I use my fingertips to call down my underwear. Sensible, nothing lacy or difficult, due to delicacy, to wash. And then I sit. Usually the coldness of the seat transforms the warning buzz to a blare, waking me, but sometimes it's the almost feeling.

"That near-miss kind of closeness. Skimming the edge. From feeling nothing's coming out, to knowing I'm at the tip of something. And if I choose to let go now, I'll never stop.

"As I wake, Phil sleeping beside me, his arms my seatbelt, I whisper the name. Void. So I extract myself from his hold, and in my conscious state, I save myself from soil. I rise to void."

SELF MEDITATING

FAY

DISSOLVE TO:

EXT. THE EAST RIVER, NEW YORK - BROOKLYN BRIDGE - MIDNIGHT

LITTLE GIRL, sitting atop the BROOKLYN-SIDE TOWER, swings her legs. FAITH, standing on the pedestrian walk, looks up. Next to the girl is an AMERICAN FLAG. The stars and the bridge lights gleam; the rest of New York—Manhattan, Brooklyn, all viewable skylines—is dark. The existing lights make the bridge glow. No human-made sounds can be heard. Below, an opaque EAST RIVER sloshes against the tower base.

> FAITH
> Hey, how about climbing down?

> LITTLE GIRL
> How about you climb up?

> FAITH
> Listen, kid, I need *you* to get on *my* level. Seniority rules.

Little girl points to the AMERICAN FLAG. She stands up, revealing a traditionally male outfit: a yellow and black Tang suit. Adding to the visual dissonance is her hair, coiled into two buns; white ruffle socks; and embroidered black flats.

> LITTLE GIRL
> Capture the flag?

> FAITH
> I'm afraid of heights.

> LITTLE GIRL
> You used to love a thrill.

Wide shot of BROOKLYN BRIDGE, carless. The two figures
dot the otherwise unbroken bridge lines.

                    FAITH
          We belong on the ground. Up in the air's
          for the birds.

                    LITTLE GIRL
          Want me to jump? Will you catch me?

                    FAITH
          No and no.

                    LITTLE GIRL
          Then capture the flag!

                    FAITH
          Sadists. They grow them young.

Ducking under a diagonal stay, Faith swings one leg
onto the safety barrier, then the other. She uses a
suspension cable to pull herself up. The safety barrier
has become her balance beam.

                    FAITH
          I'm no longer acrobatic.

                    LITTLE GIRL
          But muscles remember. Climb the
          latticework. Follow the ascending
          lights!

Wide shot of BROOKLYN BRIDGE. Faith's moving dot
appears like a spider climbing its web.

                    LITTLE GIRL
          Grab my hand. I can handle you.

                    FAITH
          Ow! Grip of iron. Someone's watched
          Mulan one too many times.

                    LITTLE GIRL
          I never asked you to be a man.

                    FAITH
          No, but you expected it.

> LITTLE GIRL
You're projecting.

> FAITH
What do you know? You're still rocking
baby teeth.

Medium shot of BROOKLYN-SIDE TOWER. A passing breeze
whips the AMERICAN FLAG into motion.

> FAITH
Well, I'm here. Now what? You climb on
my back and we monkey down?

> LITTLE GIRL
You tell me. You called for me.

> FAITH
Delusions of grandeur, little Yoda.
Why do you keep glancing at the flag?
Am I supposed to collect it and present
its spangled glory to you? Little *Cixi
Taihou*?

> LITTLE GIRL
Now who's delusional?

> FAITH
What do you want? I hate tests. Stop
swinging your legs! We're 276 feet above
the average high water. Look down!
Mistake. No, no, keep your eyes level.

> LITTLE GIRL
When you look down, what appears to you?
I see lion dances and red bean cakes.
The lady escaping the moon. Ribbons and
operas and drums. You can look without
falling.

> FAITH
No point. I know what I'd see. Bopomofo
charts. Hooked on Phonics cassette
tapes. Vocab flash cards. Times
tables. Stopwatches and long-division
worksheets.

                    LITTLE GIRL
Red and gold tinsel and China dolls and
green envelopes.

                    FAITH
Speech classes and dance and karate and
dim swing-set dreams. And you.

                    LITTLE FAITH
And me.

DEAD-END OUTLETS

HUA

"But how are *you*, Dr. Morass? By now, surely the sound of my voice induces a migraine. I feel like I'm always lecturing. Shall we switch places? Allow me to live vicariously, try on your therapist's lens.

"Part of teaching is observing. And you look in need of a good listening to. Drunk? Hardly. I argue I've never felt soberer. Punchiness does that. Though I must say, astute of you to notice a shift in my temper—what's the temperature? Rather balmy. Off goes the suit jacket. Shall I lie back, Freudian style? That's what you meant by the couch. I'll leave my shoes here. No marks, see? I call them my witching heels.

"You seem more patient when you're in a state of panic. Double meanings. How often do you question what a patient says? I.e., in your head. Ever say to yourself, 'this one sounds like a loose socket?' I think that of some of my students. Time's changed the boundaries of normal, but still I think…

"I admire your perseverance. You remind me of what I aspire to be. More automaton than human. No, you tell me what that means. I defer to the expert. All right.

"If you ask me—please suppress the urge to follow up—Phil's the one needing therapy. He's intent on remaking himself. Phil 2: Back to Bodily Youth. It's less a midlife crisis and more a sorry attempt to condition me, Pavlovian style.

"He subjects himself to those insane workouts. *And* he's hired a trainer at our gym. He'd better be overworking himself for his self. Because I care zero percent if he chisels himself into the Vitruvian Man. He assures me he's pursuing such fleshly architecture to prove that an Asian man can build mass, too. That's Asian toxic masculinity for you.

"He never voices it, but I know he thinks I desire whiteness. That I look at my sister's daughter with indirect envy. And that since I'm filled with stones instead of eggs, the closest I can get to whiteness is through fucking a white man. Because everything hinges on racial desire. Contest another abstraction.

"You deserved that PsyD. Ten out of ten for diverting the focus back to me. But please allow a wandering professor to rest.

"No, I never fall asleep on couches. Now, excuse me for my impertinence. Curiosity kills me and I've noted an absence of pictures. Your desk looks barren.

"What do *I* think about *your* lifestyle? Turning the question on the questioner. I try to avoid presumption. But I tentatively deduce that your wife left you for a younger woman. She wanted non-monogamy, the excitement and activism of youth. You tie your laces too straight. Every object in your office indicates *mise-en-scène*. Note your redundant placement of receptacles.

"Your organizer baskets house already boxed items. Clips in boxes in containers in basket drawers. I used to live in Stanford. Forget quaking; the ground here never even sneezes! But you protect these plastic organizational tools like they're keeping you together.

"You're most intimidating when you're silent. When you study your hands like that, might you be fighting the instinct to swing at me? Surely, woman to woman, you recognize that when riled, we possess the desire for violence no less than man. Perhaps we suppress the urge more due to conditioning. Tell me, do I deserve a slap?

GUANG GUAN,
BROKEN BRANCHES

I HEAR TOO MANY MEN called *guang guan*. Dead ends of family biology. Too little women to "go around." Funny how that fails, yes? Women are the rivers forward. What happens when they get evaporated? When we leave them, wipe them, trash them? One plus zero still makes one.

All that, I know. But still...

I touch my so-far life. Use my fingers to push through its hair, dive to its scalp. Back, down, deep until reaching roots. What do I find? No. What finds me?

So-cial-ize, Hua says. The dictionary entry, how unhelpful: "make (someone) behave in a way that is acceptable to their society." What about acceptable? Tell me it's okay. The command form, explicit: *you* tell me it's okay.

> **society** |səˈsīədē|
> noun
> the community of people living in a particular country or region and having shared customs, laws, and organizations.
> ORIGIN mid 16th cent. (in the sense "companionship, friendly association with others"): from French *société*, from Latin *societas*, from *socius* "companion."

From, from, from. Everything from something else. We descend. We inherit. We pass on.

Socialize. We soak our young threads in the pot. Stew, slow boil. Dyed and done. Because we grew in this pot, and birthed in this pot, even if we leave, we take the dye with us. In every pore. We sweat, bleed the dye.

I think back. My dead childhood. Unseen and unheard in best cases. In worst, the baby that everyone wanted in the dumpster. Born from a gutter, made for a dumpster. Useless girl. Because girls, like jug milk, are only good for use. For limited use. Spill, curdle, spoil, expire.

My little mind. Twisting. Realizing my "place" as a headless, tailless dragon. No fire, no voice. Only a tangled line of scales.

I never wanted a child. Never thought of a kicking belly, or a family, or a thing beyond me. This no-matter self. When you know little about yourself, why want to multiply, to copy your useless being.

Now, I think of these American women. These Chinese women. How strong and weak. Strong in new ways. Choice: open desire for self. Weak in the same old: giving up choice. Sacrificing for others. Who appreciate no sacrifices. Losing self.

Who deserves what? And when? From where? Confucius says. Auntie says. Always the monitor. Women and place. Bodies and minds.

We're the trashed blossoms. We fall from mountain trees into the dirt. Trodden by the boots of too many men without face.

Go on. Pass over us like burnt, un-sticky rice. You keep your branches broken. We keep our food warm.

PERSONA MUTA

HUA

SPEAKING IS PART OF A professor's job. Degree qualifications grant weight to the verb "profess." Avow alliance to the edification of students. Open their horizons, model the role. This pedestal's too high and sways at the whisper of a wind.

Professors profess. Writers write. Profess to write; write to profess. She does all. She never needs the microphone. Her voice carries the power of a wind turbine. Suits never fail to suit her, no shoulder pads needed. At once, she's so and un-Chinese. In the office and at the condo, her witching heels always come off. She eats while grading papers. She sends out emails and letters and testimonies, all signed with her gleaming string of degrees.

From the desk of Hua Wu Ting, the Grace Lee Boggs Professor of Law; Faculty Chair at the Center for the Study of Law and Culture, et cetera, et cetera, et cetera. Cited in numerous law journals. Interviewed by professional and popular magazines. The expert for the experts. The epitome of perfection. The model in the minority. These accolades ring hollow.

When she files her defenses, appeals to her own court of law, addresses the committees of her mind, she wants the realization of one dream. One dream, among her laundry list of dreams.

Put her on mute. No captioning. A nonspeaking role. But, also, a non-seen role. Nonentity. Cut from the party, program, scene, like all the uncelebrated actors of Asian and Pacific Islander descent. Static. White noise. Removal from all frames. Anonymous in a fame-seeking country. No one and no thing.

If the choice existed, flight or invisibility? Invisibility. Especially from those she should hold most dear. They say invisibility's the deceitful power. That a desire to be unseen indicates nefarious intentions. To have without holding, to touch without being touched.

Those who want invisibility harbor secrets. Layers within layers. Secrets within secrets.

Panopticon. She overlooks and oversees this public, professorial self from her ivory tower. Prison circle, her imprisoned selves. Welcome to the funhouse; the tricks never end. Unwilling observer to a life full of empty. Discipline and punish; punisher and prisoner. She holds herself with her own stares. The secrets boil under her skins. She never dares to set fire to her pores, to gas them out. They stay, like story pieces from a time long past.

As her niece says, everyone's a film. Stop-motion clay bits, black and white, color, Smell-O-Vision, IMAX, 3D. Motioned picture. Series of images strung together like fake pearls. Throw the necklace and beads break.

The moving pictures of longing, lonely people struggling to survive. Plateau after plateau of woe. No ending but the final credit-less end. No one sees these films. No one backs or produces them. These films remain directionless, director-less. The protagonists themselves want out. But the film always rolls. No threatening the continuity of monotony. No inserting a *deus ex machina*, a plot-thickening twist. No saving the un-savable, the unsalvageable. No triage.

What does one do when one's mouth has taken over? Body commandeered by the mechanics of the mind. One's own puppet. Walk this way, talk this way, work this way. The strings are as invisible as one wishes them to be. Endless repetition and routine. A horror musical.

Hua performs an endless masquerade. Switches from mask to mask. The watchers cheer. She steps to the beat of deadlines and dates and expectations. The rooms spin. Her essence leaves her in little breaths. Evaporation.

Whose life does she lead? Even if she could discover a way to stitch her dismembered pieces, her parted internal limbs…what then? Would she need to rise? Would they make her walk through the square? Into the judgment of the sun?

She longs for the hood of night, for a night without stars. The midnight of midnights.

Once one enters the public arena, one enters the coliseum. One must become the tigers and lions, the other gladiators. Beneath her opponents' masks are splittings of her self. The animals, she never fears. They never claim artifice for the call of blood is truth. The taste of flesh is honest; there's nothing personal in nature's kill. No psychology, just drive, instinct to survive.

What does one do when one's screaming in a soundproof room?

WHAT'S IN A SIN?

FRIDAY NIGHTS AT THE WU-TING condo usually meant watching documentaries with Fay. Sometimes Summer would join them. Jia never attended.

Enter this night. Duck under the bobbing umbrellas. Shoulder through the revolving doors. Pay the modern-day Charon, the doorman, your fare to pass to the elevator. Lift, elevate, ding.

Enter the condo. No Fay, no Summer, none but two intimate strangers. The two who became one. Phil and Hua Ting. "P" before "H," though without malicious intent.

Sit on the couch. Try to fit in the space Hua's made between. Such a small, inconsequential space—a winking line, a sliver. But one she claimed. Her wine glass, filled with "whatever you want" white wine, looks healthy. The list-trained part of her notes this glass: her third.

Watch the hoary Distinguished Professor of Systematic Theology and Christian Worldview soak up his fifteen minutes on the History Channel. Phil's hand rests on Hua's thigh. Like, Hua thinks, an elegant slug. With phalanges meant for fine motor work. She wonders what a slug with fingers would look like. Just fingers, no hands, feet, or toes. She adds a quill paintbrush to the slug's fingers. Oozy elegance, indeed.

The slug's fingers squeeze. "If we have kids, we should raise them Christian."

Hua gulps wine. "Because the academic said it's the most honorable religion?"

"I turned out well. It gave me structure. A code of morals."

Slug squeeze.

"When's the last time you went to church?"

Phil frowns. "Sin of omission."

"Others might say 'sin of commission.'"

"Must you always oppose me?"

Hua peers down into her wine glass. She hopes to find an answer, an escape, or her niece Faith. Finding none of the above, she throws back the pallid contents. She means to place the glass on the end table, but instead clatters it to rest.

"I miss us."

"*Wo bu xiang ni.*"

"You always do that. Alienate me with language. Like because I'm ancestrally Chinese I know what you mean."

"Would it be better if I switched to Taiwanese? Japanese?"

Slug fingers curl around Hua's face. "I need you here with me."

"I never left."

Slug squeeze, touch, kiss. In the background, via the next History Channel floating head, erudite droning on the sins of the forefathers.

"We could try again."

Hua becomes a listening rabbit. Still, still, whiskers twitching. Rabbit versus slug.

"You know, with different help. A surrogate. Worst-case, adoption. But only babies. You can do so much molding with them."

"If I paint over my sins, will I cleanse myself?"

"What?"

"Nothing. Just my passing thought."

COOKED STAINS

Every day, I cook for her. Food, this fake Ma of my own says, needs be fresh. Spoiled oldie.

But still I listen. On my return from massaging; assuaging; *an mo*; back-knocking, I collect best from the markets. The *lao ren* know. They point their straight-less, spot-covered fingers at me. They say, back again to cook for your Ma, ah? Just cooking doesn't make you a filial daughter. Feeding meets just one tenet. You better stay with her, keep her, respect her. No American nursing homes, ah?

I return to her. She's rearranged my place. My things, once in their place, now outplaced. In silence, I unload. But then I fix her unfixing. She grips the neck of her cane like it's a chicken for slaughter. She grips, and she watches me.

We have a new routine. We speak through the language of body. Gestures. A series of pointy looks—eyes that have eyes. Breaths from the nose, like agitated horses. Throats that can never clear. Eyes closed, lips shut, ears plugged, we know each's parameters.

I prepare. Unlike Hua, I drill-sergeant cook. All material out, in line, in best position. Wok, chopsticks, spatula. Resting plate. Metal bowls for catching. Cutting board, knives. Scallions. Garlic, ginger, always raw, no before processing. Canola, sesame oil; to coat, to taste. Yoshida sauce, red-bean paste, *la doubanjiang*, banana sauce, soy sauce.

Peel, chop, cut, set aside. Separate. Hollow-heart vegetables. Chicken slices. Woking ingredients alone. Woking together. I wok. I work. I complete. I serve. I provide rice.

She eats and I tend to my kitchen. My back reads her assessment and disapproval without needing my front.

I stained my stove. Drops of soy sauce seem brown. But when you collect all drops, when you hold them together, soy sauce is black. When you spill, splash, mistake, it leaves a brown stain. If you fail to catch early, you later find that, scrub and scrub, brownness remains. The cooking makes complete.

Ma hates cooked stains. She slapped the cooks and maids for them. Unworking hands love to slap. To feel contrast. Soft, fleshy palms against lined, taut cheeks. Looking to be hit, ah? I pay you for sloppy work? Get me a drink and then scrub!

When she finishes, I walk her to my room. Set her in my bed. In the kitchen, I see her unused seat, and I think to her.

Ma, broken audio dangles from your lips. I see you old, aged, molding. Stubborn so young. Stubborn so old. The lines of privilege rake down your sunk cheeks. Blame feeds your spirit. It feeds mine.

Do we fight because we know our secret? We share too much. We live to criticize. We hate what others call luck we won.

They say we should wear the shoes of an other. To feel other's sweat, imprint and wearing of tread-in shoes. I recall your slippers. Silk, embroidered, yellow like the sun's first morning rays. Your western furs. Always so bundled. Covered, wrapped, enveloped like New Year money, I think of you young and think of you large.

A force. Giant, rouge and lips, sparkly earrings, jade bracelets and rings and gold carats. Underneath, the silk lingerie I knew so much.

You can't remember like I do. Unwanted, uninvited. Curious to the point of desperation. In your room, on your bed, awaited your lingerie. A waiting lady. I touched. One finger, two fingers, three. Between thumb and fingers. I lifted to my face, against my cheeks. I smelled the perfume from Paris. You walked into the room with Paris on your neck, against your chest, on your wrists.

Your tread, your heels. I stole myself behind your Japanese screen. *"Jian zei, hu li wei ba!"*

You slapped me four times. Called me traitor, fox's tail. Why, you demanded.

Because I want to see you small. Your last layer. To hold you close.

And you laughed. You laughed until you sprayed me with your *kou shui*. Close? How could I get close to you?

You cared more for the cooked stains on the stove.

PINNING SAFETY

Jia

"Drew, that reminds me of time with Fay and the pins. I never told you? You know babies and their mouths.

"At six months old, when she began talking, I hoped for her to become a next Michael Kearney, but she burned up her potential. Misleading promise of youth, ah?

"I wanted for her to remember her roots. Prepare her. Too much whitewashing in school, even nursery and pre-K. So I signed her for baby Chinese folk dance. Such small costumes. Difficult detail sewing.

"I tended to lunch for *one* second. When I turned to her, I see her open my case of safety pins—and swallow some like seeds! I first thought she must be stupid, but no, I see Fay's eyes flash.

"That morning she refused to eat. She force me to force her. I expected crying, but she never used crying when upset. And then I thought, all those hours later, she forgot.

"Children remember more than we think. They catalog and tally and make score due to feelings. Without words to voice, feelings mold memories that turn to fired clay.

"Fay's eyes told me. She swallowed the pins to create vengeance. Rebellious, even at six months.

"Terrible emergency visit. All those nurses and doctors judged me. Fay wanted to shame me like I shamed her. Like we, parent and child, were equals!

"When I put her to crib, I took out the safety pins from hospital. I wondered what swallowing safety pins meant. Because the Chinese think of fate. Of intent. Nothing can be accidents.

"Why swallow safety pins? On my sewing table needles, ribbons, thimble, buttons, thread. Plenty to swallow. Why open my case of pins?

"I knew. She seen me with the pins. Fixing, holding cloth to cloth. Placeholder, temporary marriage of materials. I smacked her hand when she tried to touch. Open or closed, I keep them away.

"Who named them safety pins? Where's safety? There's only metal. Hinge. Open to find little stabber. Sticking the pin. Close to secure, hide the point.

"I think she swallowed herself. Even so young, Fay surprised everyone. Too many layers under her sheath. She still hides her stabber. Sharp mind and tongue, ejected when least expected. It hurts to swallow her words.

"When I cut her off now, I do it for me. She hurts me. Become a stranger to me. To hear her stings. I dream of pinning her in the safe spaces. I know she makes decisions that lead nowhere for use. Hua tells me, her life, not yours. She grown. Know your new place.

"What madness! What can my daughter know? She's mine. *I* made her. She owes me safety. I need to pin her to me. But more I try, more I fail. More I see us unravel, from cloth to thread."

SELF MEDITATING

Fay

DISSOLVE TO:

EXT. THE EAST RIVER, NEW YORK - BROOKLYN BRIDGE
- MIDNIGHT

LITTLE FAITH, standing atop the BROOKLYN-SIDE TOWER,
waves her arms. FAITH, sitting on the AMERICAN FLAG
STAND, looks down. As before, the night owns the city.
The two are alone together.

> LITTLE FAITH
> Pull me up or lift yourself down.

> FAITH
> You ever stop with the demands?

> LITTLE FAITH
> That's what bothers you most. You can't
> control me. You can't control what you
> feel. What you want. What do you want?

> FAITH
> You, out of my head!

Little Faith whips out a ribbon bouquet. She flicks
her wrist and the ribbon unfurls in a fury of red. In
a blink, she uses the ribbon as a lasso. She lands on
Faith's lap and they look down on the dead city.

> LITTLE FAITH

You want to suffocate me.

Faith wraps the tail of the AMERICAN FLAG around their
legs. The red and white stripes clash with their yellow
and black clothing.

> LITTLE FAITH
> You want to become untouchable, even
> to yourself. I ate fear to survive. I

learned to use the feelings to simply
become. You think you've learned your
best management practices. No touch, no
risk. You think you know.

> FAITH
> I know nothing.

> LITTLE FAITH
> Truth. You shirk me because I'm truth.
> Worse, I'm *your* truth. What empowers
> your art?

> FAITH
> Lies.

> LITTLE FAITH
> You document. You search for the
> mislabeled lies. The lies that're really
> truths. Your documentation seeks the
> mess in the closet. The dirt under the
> rug. The cells beneath the surface.

> FAITH
> Such a baby Buddha. The faith in youth.

> LITTLE FAITH
> There's a space between us. You should
> hold there.

Little Faith flicks and the red ribbon tongues out, out
toward the Manhattan side of the bridge. When fully
extended, the ribbon hovers in the air, a red path
above a black-lit bridge.

> LITTLE FAITH
> You think your extreme works for you.
> That it's the best style of being.
> That you must protect, self-cordon to
> preserve yourself. That you're incapable
> of generating multiple selves. Of
> regenerating.

> FAITH
> What's the use in changing a working
> system?

                    LITTLE FAITH
What's the sense in wanting? I know your
answer before you thought it out. No
sense in wanting. Senselessness.

                    FAITH
To want means to build to a breakdown.

                    LITTLE FAITH
You follow up but never follow through.
You dabble. You pretend you're a lost
girl when you're a grown woman. You
know your wants. You pretend they never
existed. That's the depth of your lie.
You think you lie to be true.

                    FAITH
Denial never killed anyone.

The two stare at the red path. Little Faith leaps off
Faith's lap and steps onto the flag stand. She extends
her arms laterally, making buzzing airplane sounds, and
dips one foot in front of the other.

                    FAITH
You trying to kill yourself?
Retroactively kill me? Come back.

Little Faith buzzes louder. Her voice amplifies and
echoes, as if she's hooked up to mismatched speakers.
She runs before somersaulting onto the midpoint of
the hanging ribbon. It holds firm, a bridge supported
by nothing. Little Faith, holding up her arms in a
gymnastic finish, turns to face Faith.

                    LITTLE FAITH
More than what meets your eyes.

                    FAITH
You're crazy. You think the impossible
and believe your thoughts will make it
real. You want the world and think it'll
accept and love you. I can't lie, I
enjoy breaking bubbles. I love breaking
it to you, specifically. Because you
need to know that the world expects the
world from you. And you can never expect

anything in return. Nothing positive,
anyway.

Faith stands up, holding onto the American Flag's POLE.
Little Faith yawns and settles into a straddle split,
chin in her hands.

> FAITH
> Little girl, they live to destroy
> dreamers like you. In all possible ways.
> Want to know the universe of pain and
> sorrow just a safety pin away from your
> heels?

Faith shakes the AMERICAN FLAG. It rattles. She plucks
it from the stand. With one hand grasping the stand for
balance, she holds the flag out. There's no wind, so its
length hangs limp, like a rag.

> FAITH
> Pioneering America. The Fearless
> American Spirit. Land of dreamers, dream
> chasers, dream catchers. Catch and
> release to destroy. Glory be liberty,
> self-evident truths, and the Great White
> Man. Where do you think you fit in?
> Neither here, nor there, but in between?
> In between the in between? You think
> they'll make room for you, something
> so unfathomably unconventional? (Yes,
> something: the question is What are
> you.) They still selectively acknowledge
> humanity. You break from their model
> minority myth to rail against violence
> done to people browner than you—then
> what? You think you own a voice? Own
> *your* voice, let alone your mind and
> body? Peer between your little legs and
> check those freckles and slants in the
> mirror. Your existence is supposedly
> impossible, so you're shunned or
> rendered invisible.

Little Faith, still split-sitting, watches Faith
brandish the flag.

                    FAITH
Of course, everything's relative. We
relate to what we know. We relay our
knowns. Yes, we could be subject to more
injustice. But in this American context,
take all your grand plans and chuck
them off this bridge. Bury them in the
East River. Save yourself the hurt and
disappointment. There's nothing worse
than disappointment.

                    LITTLE FAITH
Expect disappointment and never hope?
How do you sustain yourself?

Tired, Faith inserts the flag back into its stand. She
leans against the pole.

                    FAITH
A necessary course of mental action.
Deliver us from frustration. I
lied. There's something worse than
disappointment. Impotence.

                    LITTLE FAITH
Without hope, what's the point in
living?

                    FAITH
Because suicide means they automatically
win. We're guaranteed misery and death.
But we control whether we allow hope
to creep in. Eat what little control
comes your way. Eat it, swallow it
whole before someone steals your meager
sustenance.

                    LITTLE FAITH
A hopeless existence sounds like a
lonely one. A connectionless one.

                    FAITH
You can't survive on dreams. You'll
fade. Layer by layer, you'll melt into
air.

Little Faith stands up on the red ribbon.

                    LITTLE FAITH
          Join me, for a try?

                        FAITH
          No. I know the outcome. I don't believe
          in magic. I'd walk on, and we'd both
          fall. Too much weight on a path backed
          by nothing.

TURN THE PHRASE

Hua

WHILE IT'S HAPPENING, SHE LOOKS at his eyebrows. They're fine, like shaved flakes of cheese. Except black. Especially moldy cheese, perhaps. Or the kind that's supposed to be moldy because that's its specialty.

Because he always complains about the eye contact. How he needs her focus, how she must join her pupils to his. She remembers helping Jia find "pupil" in the dictionary. Origins in late Middle English. Derived, the entry read, from the Old French, *"pupille,"* or the Latin *pupilla*. Pupil, the black circular opening, the diminutive of *pupa*, "doll." And the selection of "doll," due to the small, reflected images perceived to be seen by the eye. Captured, encapsulated by eyes. But there's also pupil, the student, willing consumer of knowledge. From where and whom is this knowledge absorbed? All those pupils watching, watching for data that will shape their perceptions and actions.

Are you into this? Are you here with me? Are you paying attention?

Sweat drops derived from his forehead pelt her face. He's spitting on her in every possible way, figuratively and metaphorically. A pupil needs a teacher. Two teachers can never be. One needs relegation, degradation, submission. She hates forced learning. She misses her agency.

The motions, the reactions, he's instructed her to perform these. Implicitly and explicitly. Through the command of voice and body and expectation. She thinks of the last time she and a colleague took a spin class.

Instructor language: faster; push harder. That all you can give? Work like you mean it! Put yourself into it. Let's see you surpass your comfort zone. Beauty's pain, women!

She's become his skin bike. Ridden skin, razed insides. The hurt lives and swells inside. Vessel body. Conduit for his revelation. He wears her in and out, on and over, with endurance.

The odd fact: She knows better. She participates because she's tired of arguing. Her excuses sound flat to her own ears. No thanks. Feeling unlike you. Out of the mood. Rejection's a bitch for the provider and receiver.

Oh, she knows why. Why she's never feeling like that. And the reason beneath the tabletop of her mind, the seed inside the seedless grape... stays. If she said it, if she extracted the root from that self, would she rip out her complaisance, too? She tethered her center to complaisance.

She's waiting: an endurance game. How funny, the etymology of the word. Endurance, "capacity" to "last or to withstand wear and tear." How much can one handle? Can one take into oneself? What's the expiration date on "continued existence, ability to last"?

Obsolete, absolution. She no longer wanted the power of acceptance. She wanted the acquiescence of rejection. She wanted. She wanted outside the lines. She wanted crushing release. No! She desired. But did she deserve desire? Did that matter? When had desire become an entitlement? The pursuit of desire—did it lead to pursuing happiness?

Back to the eyebrows, fine and disarrayed. Like faded lines of ink. Attenuated by derivations. Passed from son to son through a stream of subjugated daughters. Fold into the collapse. Speed the removal.

WHEN LIGHT
MET SHADOW

Fay

LIGHT THRIVED IN THE CITY. She felt needed. Everyone used her because they never slept.

They worshiped and praised her. Just turn on the light, they'd say, and everything's better. All's right in the light. Writers write. Teachers teach. Workers work. Lovers love.

But for some time, Light felt...dim. She consulted technician after technician, electrician after electrician, but no one located the waning of brightness that she felt. Brighten up, they'd say, beaming under her glow. Your filament's fine.

Light tried. She tried to live up to her name. For the name's sake, for the sake of the people who used and needed her. She forced herself to feel the lightness others expected from her.

Perhaps she could've faked until the feeling felt real, or real enough. Time, she'd heard them say, enabled many improbabilities. Like breaking in fresh shoes, or wearing someone down to be on your side, the persevering drum of time eventually made resistance futile. In like a light, on like a light, ongoing like a light. Bulb that never dies.

But then came the birds. Dying. Dying because of all the light they couldn't stop seeing. Jewel-toned skyscrapers, lit from her electric flame, scraping the winged beings from existence.

Night flights. The fall migration became a migrating fall. Over every big city, Light and her counterparts disoriented birds to the death. She watched or heard them die. Sometimes, a *boom* or *splat* against transparently clean windows. Other times, they drew concentric circles with their wings, spiraling in confusion. Always, the falls. From low or great heights, down, ground out by the unforgiving gravel.

Hummingbird, Thrush, Warbler, Sparrow. The ground became a littered haven for burnt-out feathers, for snapped wings and crushed bird bodies.

Yes, the sight frightened the people. But the smell of decay and the blackness of old blood peeled the people's eyelids. Mayors across the country pounded fists against podiums. A solution hatched.

Lights Out. Turn off the excess. Provide the birds with the stars of night. Let the natural gems light a trail from nesting to wintering ground. Let nature do its work.

And so it happened. For the first time, they shut off parts of Light. She breathed these parts into rest. And these parts, they learned what it meant to go dark. To switch off. To be…nothing.

Oddly, in the absence of complete illumination, Light recognized more. The spaces in between. Cracks, corners, turns, tears. And the chasms, they failed to frighten her. She viewed them as a platform to another, deeper level of understanding. She lingered, waiting for a moment. Waiting for the living of a moment. To live one moment.

On an ordinary night during Lights Out, the moment arrived.

Under the north side of St. Patrick's Cathedral, over the bronze rippling back of Atlas. Between the surfaces and pockets of her danced dark shapes. Partial darkness and partial lightness met. Intercepting building bodies and reaching tree limbs cast opaque regions. Suddenly these dark images, the shaded parts of pictures, eclipsed Light's city.

Light looked for an explanation from the people. But no one noticed. The never-sleeping people continued living. Writing, teaching, working, loving. They continued to cling to the parts of her they could keep on.

She followed the unilluminating entities. Always between, under, beneath. Never out in the complete open. Always changing shapes. The closer she drew, the more they all pulled away. Wait, she cried, wait! Let me touch you. Let me hold you. But the second she held out her rays, lit the between, they dispersed, fleeing her touch.

The more she followed and studied the dark, evanescent blankets, the more she realized. They'd existed all along. Her overpowering presence had denied, muted, silenced them into hiding.

Light followed the outlines to the City's underground. Down the stairs, past the buzzing people, down to the ghost stations. To City Hall, in all its abandoned glory. Light hadn't been fully used here since December of 1945. She streamed through the tile arches, via spider-loved chandeliers, through cracks in the blacked-out skylights. It smelled of musts. The must of a worldly war. The must of disuse.

But she felt, for the first time, a minority. The shades, their shifting shapes, *they* thrived here. She felt outdone, out-sung, outside of in. And interested in this new feeling. This strangeness. Attracted to her inadequacy. To its possibilities.

They swirled, they contoured, they traced her outlines. Could they speak? They whispered across her. The in-between areas. What a lurking nature. What velvety texture. She felt the quiet hunger of desire. For more, for midpoints, for something other than. Light learned to stay still. To withdraw from the outward. To rein in her rays.

A silhouette, the largest of them all, sidled up to her. It spoke, voice like a cat's tongue—rough like sandpaper, but pleasantly sensual.

I'm what you've been missing, it murmured. The bottomless hole. The edges beyond vision. The blur between object and surface. The bounce back. I've been living in your peripheries. I can't exist without the interplay of you.

It drew back and forth dark, intangible tides. And spoke again. We dance, you and I. But we can never truly meet. Instead, we forever dance the paso doble. You charge, I draw back. You recede, I push forward. I'm in you. In your soul. In your soles. You eat me. You feed me. We feed off each other. I'm the hint of what could be. What must be. I linger in the potential.

Light pulsed. So we live together but by being apart?

Yes.

And we must never meet?

Yes. Because we'll never meet as equals. Nothing's ever equal. No one's equal. But now that you know me, you'll remember me. When you dim, I define myself. When you die, I live. We each tip the balance of the other.

RICE PRETZEL BARREL

Fay

BLACK SCREEN:

No sound. Then, static.

FADE IN:

Abrupt medium close-up of BROKEN PRETZEL RODS, scattered on scuffed tiles. No other visual distractions.

> FAITH (V.O.)
> When little girl graduates from eating applesauce to apples, she discovers pretzels.

CUT TO:

Black. Sound of hands breaking pretzels.

> FAITH (V.O.)
> Her mom refuses to spend money like the American-born mothers. Ma wears "cheap" as an honorable badge. When the Chinese ladies hold sales at the market, she buys in bulk. Buy two get one free. Buy one get one. Super sale! Or, as they all pronounce it, shoo-per sale.

FADE IN:

Pan from sale sign to sale sign. Numbers and Chinese characters in red, and the Chinglish translations below, in black. Sound of different overlapping dialects, cacophony.

CUT TO:

Black. Sound of hands breaking pretzels.

                    FAITH (V.O.)
          Though a toddler, little girl never
          toddles. She strides the aisles like her
          mom. They spend hours hunting for the
          best deals. And when rice goes on sale,
          they buy as many bags as Ma can shove
          into her half-latched suitcase.

FADE IN:

Groceries on a running conveyor belt. Beeping of the
register. Butcher-glove-enclosed hands of the checkout
lady. Bags in bags, crinkling of thin plastic. Heaving
of sacks of rice. And amid the chicken feet, the bok
choy, the Dragon Eye, the lone barrel of pretzels.

                                              CUT TO:

Black. Sound of hands breaking pretzels.

                    FAITH (V.O.)
          When they toil home, rumbling through
          the streets wet with liquids and brown
          with dirt unknown, little girl thinks
          of what's next. Unpacking. Yelling.
          Slipping. Tearing. Pulling.

FADE IN:

Abrupt medium close-up of broken pretzel rods,
scattered on scuffed tiles. Zoom out to reveal TORN RICE
SACK, on its side. Mounds of rice mix with shards of
pretzel.

                    FAITH (V.O.)
          Ma rages in their ninety-square-foot
          apartment, screams until the neighbors
          take a broom handle to the wall. She
          retires to bed and makes a tent of the
          covers.

                                              CUT TO:

Black. Sound of hands breaking pretzels.

                    FAITH (V.O.)
          Little girl makes cleaning a game.
          Unlike the other children, she owns
          no touch-me books. The rice and the
          pretzels on the cracked tile—these
          become a live-action tactile book.

FADE IN:

Close-up of a pile of broken pretzel rods, contrasted
with a next-door pile of rice.

                    FAITH (V.O.)
          Little girl loves the feel of uncooked
          rice. Smooth and hard, she thinks of
          them as oblong pearls. They smell like
          promises. Then, the pretzels.

Extreme close-up of broken pretzel rods, white innards
contrasted with brown shells. Close-up of salt grains.
They look like rocky pebbles.

                                              CUT TO:

Black. Sound of hands breaking pretzels.

                    FAITH (V.O.)
          She wears the salt on her tongue. She
          scoops the biggest, whole-est pretzel
          pieces into Ziploc bags, and nibbles
          on the smallest broken bits. She's been
          trained to love the bitter, the sour,
          the broken. Little girl thinks the
          whitest crumbs taste like sawdust. They
          cling to her throat, a layer of sand.
          She prefers the salt.

FADE IN:

Close-up of the pretzel barrel, now filled with rice.

                    FAITH (V.O.)
          The repurposed pretzel barrel is heavy.
          Little girl reaches inside to dig her
          hands into the grains. They're cool

against her clammy palms. Ma is sleeping
or sulking.

Close-up of hands sifting through uncooked rice.

>   FAITH (V.O.)
>   When the other neighbors start making
>   the strangled noise, little girl wraps
>   her arms and legs around the rice
>   pretzel barrel. Either the barrel's
>   small, or she's large. Regardless, they
>   fit in this plastic-girl embrace. She
>   balances salt pebbles on her cheeks and
>   pretends they're tears. She tries to
>   catch them in her mouth.

                                              CUT TO:

Black. Moment of silence.

>   FAITH (V.O.)
>   Faster than a sack of rice can split,
>   little girl will grow. From girl to
>   woman. She will encounter larger breaks.
>   She will be unable to place these
>   remains in proper receptacles. She will
>   be unable to wrap herself around the
>   solutions, if any exist.
>
>   Woman will buy her own bags of rice,
>   sometimes at full price. She will stop
>   in the snack aisle, and gaze at the
>   barrels of different pretzels. Nuggets,
>   twists, sticks, rods. They'll wear
>   different sizes and shapes of salt. Her
>   mouth will water. Parchment mouth, dune
>   throat. She might reach out and run her
>   fingers over the decorative bumps in the
>   plastic. She might lift a barrel into
>   her arms, cradle its weight against her
>   thin bosom.
>
>   But woman will return the barrel to its
>   shelf, to sit with its sisters. She will
>   look at the barrel she touched and look

at the empty corner in her cart. But she
will turn and push away.

When she returns to the ninety-square-
foot apartment, she'll unpack. Next
door, a couple will curse at each other.
Objects thrown, hit or missed targets,
land. Next door, throbbing music,
running booze, yelling undergrads. Woman
will take kitchen shears and cut three
inches off the corner of a rice bag.
She will scoop five uncooked cups into
her cooker, and she'll add six cups of
water. With a clip, she'll close the
hole she created.

Sound of hands breaking pretzels.

LI BU CONG XIN: SPIRIT WILLING, FLESH WEAK

HUA

"THE OTHER DAY I WENT to the salon. So someone with knowing hands could trim my split ends.

"I've always been, as Jia puts it, 'wasteful' when it comes to hair. I pay too much for too little return. Nothing much to show the world, she thinks. I'm sure she's right, to an extent. You want to give and receive in equal measures. Ideally, anyway. Because we all lie to ourselves: there's always a settler, and always a reacher. A compromise, a drawn settlement.

"At the salon, I thought about why I pay sixty dollars for the same corkscrew-curled blonde woman to trim an inch off the ends of my hair. Every four weeks, the same deal. I sink into the same leather chair.

"Denise—we're on a forename basis—laces her fingers through my hair. Roots to tips. Turns the water on. The water's so close the gush echoes. She asks me about my work, my students, my impending articles. But it's like sitting in the dentist's chair. We owe each other nothing. Denise asks out of decorum. I respond in the same way.

"Neither of us is paying utmost attention to the other. She's scratching my scalp with last week's frustrations with the backs of her pointy false nails. They remind me of the fingernail guards popular during the Qing Dynasty. The longer the fingernail guard, the higher the status. Anyway, I'm taking it. Because it hurts, but it's necessary. I feel the dead cells relinquish their hold.

"We move into the next phase. Her touches become soft, cradling. She's careful to prevent shampoo and conditioner from bleeding into my eyes. Denise marvels at the 'natural softness' of my hair. At its 'envious straightness.' I tell myself she's intelligent. It's true. Just a different intelligence than I'm used to. I find her frankness soothing, an aloe vera against the academic smoke I've fumbled my way through.

"I smell like chemical coconut and mango. I avoid thinking of Taiwan. Of my father, and especially of Jia and my mother. Denise guides me to another bottom-sucking chair. She puts stiletto to the pedal. Pump, pump, pump, hiss of air as the seat adjusts. I wonder why stylists always wear stilettos, especially since they're on their feet all day. For the performance aspect? For whom? But she tells me to relax and stop thinking. I try.

"Denise starts the cutting routine. Comb the tangles until they die. Surrounded by sheets of black strands, I look like a Chinese ghost in an opera. But for one section, she pins back my hair. Now I feel like a doll. All I need is rouge.

"Down the comb strokes, with teeth like fingers. Snip, snip, snip. Scissors chomp. Next section. Repeat the repetition. I hear the strands fall, and it's a release. I see the black bits fanned out on the white floor. And I want more, but I sit and wait.

"She blow-dries my hair and straightens it while we laugh at the gesture. I see myself through the vanity. And she brandishes a hand-held mirror so I can behold the back of my head.

"I hold my metallic card out to her, and our fingers slip against each other during the handoff. She rings me up and I know. I know why it's sixty dollars. I'll continue paying. I can't afford to stop.

"Denise provides me with a service. Our monthly interactions are indubitably transactional. I'm just another client. She's just another cosmetologist.

"But she gives me more. And in the time and space we share, I take it. Because I know what'll happen, and I let it unfold. Petal by petal, strand by strand. These trims are safe cuts. Safe shedding. Denise handles me. Under the glaring salon lights, jazz playing in the background, I allow vulnerability in. Far from an embrace—I shake its hand.

"Okay, doctor. I told you how I feel. I suppose you'll ask me for a dream next. I anticipate you now. Does that make you nervous, doctor? Do you feel exposed?

"Some post-haircut nights, a dream visits. Nightmare? You decide. Or ask me to decide.

"I stand in front of our full-length mirror. And I strip. One boot, two. One stockinged foot, two. Roll down the pants. (I pile everything, stable on bottom, fragile on top; I've never been messy.) Blazer off. Dress shirt off. Bracelet and earrings and that left-hand ring. Underwear, bottom and top.

"Bare, but for my hair curtain. My down-to-elbows coverage.

"I find scissors in my hands. Then I'm cutting, chopping, hacking off the split, dead ends. But it's not enough. I feel the need clawing out from behind my throat. From my esophagus and trachea. Gullet and windpipe. Visceral, heaving feeling.

"A razor's in my hands. I lift it. And I raze. I shave. I buzz and it's the sound of finality, of falling. Hair slams to the floor, landlocked. My head becomes an egg. I've never been so afraid. But I've never been so brave. And I look. In my bared state, I am *jolie laide*, beautiful ugly."

PERFORMANCE REVIEW

HUA

PHIL steps inside HUA's office and closes the door behind him.

HUA

(Looking up) Feel free to come in.

PHIL

An inconvenient time?

PHIL moves an armchair over to HUA's desk and sits, leaning back, arms draped on the armrests.

HUA

For you, it's never an inconvenient time.

HUA takes out a lens wipe and cleans her glasses. She puts them back on and slides forward on her chair, leaning her crossed arms on the desk.

PHIL

Waiting for the perfect—

HUA

This opportunity means…as I'm sure you know, everyone raves about you.

PHIL crosses his ankle over his knee.

PHIL

If this were a paper, I'd write "delineate" here. But we've always had different teaching styles.

HUA

> (*Too quietly for him to hear*) A JD. in ego.

> *A beat.*

> I remember the first horror film I watched. My first
> year in America. A B-grade, made-for-TV movie. The
> title never made it to memory. But that opening
> sequence…

> *PHIL picks up a book on HUA's desk, flipping
> through the many passages she's bookmarked.*

HUA

> The movie opened with a teen girl's dream. But
> viewers are fooled—it's shot without surrealism.
> Family members sing this girl the birthday song.
> The usual. She blows out the candles, face
> shining. Everyone claps.

> Family pass out plates. She's now a big girl. A
> young woman capable of cutting cake.

PHIL

> (*Glancing up from the book*) You highlight too much.

HUA

> We see the cake. It's a POV shot; we see through
> the girl's eyes. A well-decorated cake. Delicate,
> intricate flowers atop layers of icing. Looks sweet
> enough to make you suck your cheeks. To make your
> tongue hurt. A sugar-punch in the mouth.

PHIL

> You've always harbored a desire to keep
> everything. Like you're in a perpetual state of
> starvation.

HUA

> Then the camera focus shifts. We're distanced
> viewers again. We watch her take the knife, and

poise it over the top of the cake. Between two
flowers, an ideal space for the first cut.

*HUA opens a desk drawer and pulls out a letter
opener. Her motions carry out her descriptive
speech.*

PHIL

Odd, considering how you've never wanted
for anything. Perhaps we remember ancestral
lacks. That's what Jia would say, no? Buddhist
doublespeak.

HUA

She hovers over the cake, hands unsure. Then she
moves, resting the knife's teeth. It's kissing the
cake's top. There's a moment. The breath before
the dive. The look before the jump. The lightning
before the thunder.

HUA brings the letter opener down.

The cut. We expect a filling of some kind. A mousse.
Cream. More icing. Chocolate, vanilla, strawberry.

But it's blood. All this red oozing, oozing. One
deep cut and the red's out. On her hands, soaking
the white tablecloth, eating the cake inside out.
She's screaming while the family silently watches.

She screams herself awake to a sweating body and a
white-sheeted bed. That's when I turned the TV off.
Nightmares for a month afterward. That year I had
ice cream for my birthday.

PHIL

(Tossing the book onto the desk) And you think
too much. At work. At home. Without or with me.
Cerebral.

HUA

Your layers surprised me. Rather, how you lack
them.

PHIL spreads his legs, leaning forward to rest his elbows on his knees.

HUA

You're taking this so well.

A beat.

We're codependent. Vampiric. You're so American, but you want the Chinese wife. You want your cake to split itself open, again and again, and feed itself to you.

PHIL

You're a dead fish. Nothing stimulates you.

HUA stands up and takes her glasses off.

HUA

Kiss me.

PHIL stands up. He pulls HUA up and over her side of the desk, plopping her down on the edge closest to him. He pulls HUA's head back by her bun and kisses her.

At the moment of contact, HUA stabs PHIL in the gut with the letter opener. She rotates the blade like she's turning a screw. HUA withdraws her face and PHIL's hands from her hair and neck.

PHIL coughs, choking, and they both look down at the blood.

HUA

This is what I imagine while you're nailing me.

PERFORMED REVIEW

JIA

MY TURN. I SPEAK IN English. Impeccable English. Because the language of the hands, of pressing hands into skin is universal. You demand a massage, so I'll give you one. Provide you this service, free of charge. But that's a lie. No thing's ever free. I must take something from you.

You, mother, yes, you, gave birth to me. These fingertips trace the origins of their prints back to you. You pushed me into being. No me without you. No me without him. I push out your pain with hands descended from your cells. We share pieces of the same skin, hide in a similar hide.

"Parent," too, sprung from an origin. The Latin verb "*parere*," a "bringing forth." You say I create the bodily tension you're feeling. Your body's twisted, inside and out, because of me. You're beholden to the pain, and I'm beholden to you. I must take away what I've caused.

I'm parent to your aches and creaks. You want me to kill these wayward children. My hands—partly your hands—attack your brittle back. My fists—your fists—drum your rolled skin. I play a death march, play you into silence. You never say if my force hurts you.

On an average day, you frustrate me. But at your best, I'm at my worst. I want to chop through your neck like a Grandmaster chops a block. Chop without mess. Kill you in two. Bury your master mind and that evil mouth separately.

During my childhood, long before the appearance of your wrinkles and hairy moles and mottled skin, you spoke of an only child, a boy. His mother treated him like the last emperor. Spoiled him until rotten eggs cringed at his touch. Whenever the outside world blamed him for wrongdoing, she'd roll up her shirt and say, drink my milk. You'll remember, *bao bei*, my love, and feel safe. She did so until he left the house.

Imagine, you said, a man at his mother's breast. This boy-man found the world an ocean, and he neither knew how to swim, nor had a vessel or raft. After a humiliating scene with his boss, boy-man killed him. At the trial, all agreed the boy-man must die. What's your last wish, they asked. I want my mother's milk, he said. She rolled up her shirt, to show her shriveled, milk-less breasts, and he bent his head. He put the nipple into his mouth, and then onlookers heard her scream. Blood spurted, soaked her silk shirt. He held her nipple between his teeth—and then spat it onto the floor.

Bao bei, my only son, why hurt me so, she cried, gawking hole oozing where her nipple had sagged. Boy-man stood and, judging strangers watching, jumped up and down on the detached mammary duct. He stomped the nipple into nonexistence. Then he bent and looked his mother in her crying eyes. You deserved that, he said, because you never taught me.

I studied this story until I could tell it better than you. Until I could predict your story-tied intonations and gestures. No mercy or exceptions for me, no coddling. Did I want to end up like nipple-tearing boy-man? Did I want to shame my family? No matter that I'm female—girl, even worse! One slip, and you become a whore or slave. All different names for the same place and role.

My hands have delivered you. On this massage table, you snore. Release, muscle redemption. My hands, brought forth from you. But you never nursed me. I drank from Nanny. I tumbled from your body, but from that moment onward, I took nothing of you. You injected your judgment into me. You shamed me into shaming myself. Worthless girl, you scathed, and I repeated the words, mouthed them till I fell asleep.

I could take your hands in mine. Your arthritic-bound hands. We could link hands. And I could lift our hands to your face. To your deflated cheeks, so empty without their rouge. We could crawl down your jowls to your lazy jugular. Four hands. Two parents, two children. Two pairs could curl around your tired beat.

You'd never wake. Together, we could withdraw the breaths from you. We could bring forth the last breath. No final shudder or sucking. An exhale, quiet, like the air created by the water oxen's fly-batting tail.

I want to return you. Send you back. With you, every month is the Ghost Festival. You're my living demon, forked, hanging tongue. The body you inhabit agrees with me. You should disintegrate, becoming shadow. Without a mouth, you own no voice. You can think me to death, but I'll never hear.

When I move you to your bed, my hands curl your body to my breast. Without dentures, you have no teeth to bite me. I never taught you how to treat me. Am I to blame? I respond to your thousand cuts. Out of habit. Because I've no imagination for what I haven't experienced.

The bed beneath you is a twin-less twin. Your wasting body seems to apologize for even taking up a third of the mattress. Once, during the days of the General, you were the Taiwanese Marilyn Monroe. Your skin remembers, ebbing and flowing where it used to stretch over muscle.

You breathe in puffs, in between snores. I hold our hands to your nose and feel the air escape. And I place these hands on your neck. I make a necklace with my fingers, your skinfolds undulating in awareness. But I never make it a choker. Because you're my *baoru*, and I'm stuck with this burden.

REVIEWED PERFORMANCE

Fay

DISSOLVE TO:

**EXT. THE EAST RIVER, NEW YORK - BROOKLYN BRIDGE
- MIDNIGHT**

LITTLE FAITH is standing at the base of the MANHATTAN-
SIDE TOWER. FAITH, lying on a bench, gestures her over.

>   LITTLE FAITH
>   Party for two. Or two's a party?

>   FAITH
>   I don't remember being you.

>   LITTLE FAITH
>   You always tried to choose your
>   memories. As if the sky could choose its
>   stars. When they shine. When they dim.
>   When they fall in burning glory. Or when
>   they simply wink out.

Little Faith sits on Faith's feet. Faith tugs her legs
free and huddles them to her chest.

>   FAITH
>   Getting married tonight? Thought we were
>   hoping to move past child brides.

Faith scrutinizes Little Faith's Qing dynasty—style dress.
Little Faith also sports a phoenix-crown headdress.

>   LITTLE FAITH
>   Are you more phoenix than dragon? Or vice
>   the verse? More yin than yang? More earth,
>   dark, cold? Less heaven, heat, light?

>   FAITH
>   You know better than to drink from the
>   East River. Heavy pollution, I hear,
>   perhaps comparable to the Hudson.

Little Faith holds her hands up, "surrender" style.

> LITTLE FAITH
> Mirror me. *Dong bu dong?*

> FAITH
> What's there to understand?

Little Faith stands; Faith reluctantly follows suit.

> LITTLE FAITH
> *Xiao laoshu shang dengtai.*

> FAITH
> You expect me to remember the gestures?
> You're notably closer to nursery days.

> LITTLE FAITH
> As *Ayi* taught us. *Dong bu dong*? Repeat
> after me. *Xiao laoshu shang dengtai.*

> FAITH
> There was a little mouse climbing up a
> lamp stand.

> LITTLE FAITH
> *Tou chi you.*

> FAITH
> He stole and ate some oil. Wait, what
> animal eats oil? A suicidal one?

> LITTLE FAITH
> *Xia bu lai.*

> FAITH
> He wasn't able to get down. Serves him
> right.

> LITTLE FAITH
> *Miao miao miao, mao lai la.*

> FAITH
> I refuse to meow. A cat came along.

> LITTLE FAITH
> *Jiligulu gun xialai.*

                    FAITH
        "Rumble," the mouse fell off the lamp.
        And presumably the cat ate him. Where
        are you going now?

Little Faith stops in front of a colorfully decorated
section of the bridge.

                    FAITH
        Am I supposed to explain what these are?
        How much of what I know do you know?

                    LITTLE FAITH
        Up to you.

                    FAITH
        I'm afraid you know all I know and more.

                    LITTLE FAITH
        Zhi ji zhi bi.

                    FAITH
        Bu dong.

                    LITTLE FAITH
        Know thyself; know thy enemy.

Little Faith removes a condom and a tampon from the
bridge's latticework. She begins to put the two
together when Faith snatches both. Faith throws the
objects into the estuary.

                    FAITH
        Buyao name zuo! When's the last time the
        Department of Transportation cleaned
        here? Love locks indeed. Come, help me
        remove the trash. No touching anything
        that looks like your first selections—let
        me handle those.

The two walk down the line of locks, collecting trash
bags, hair scrunchies, panties, bras, and other
personal effects. They create a pile next to a nearby
bench.

                    LITTLE FAITH
        Couples lock their love to this

bridge. Throw away the key to the
waterway.

> FAITH
> No, just a symbol of their love. The
> key sinks to the bottom. No purchasing
> buoyancy.

Little Faith reaches into her headdress and pulls out a
bobby pin. She picks a heart-shaped lock and lifts it from
the bridge. The pair returns to the bench to examine it.

> FAITH
> A heart-shaped lie.

> LITTLE FAITH
> A promise.

> FAITH
> Made and lost, forgotten like its
> corresponding key. Buried beneath silt
> and clay and rubble and rocks. Maybe
> swallowed by a curious fish. If fish can
> live in such pollution.

Little Faith presses the heart-shaped lock into Faith's
hands.

> FAITH
> Heavier than it looks. Heart stone.
> Locked in a stone heart. Stone-heart
> lock. Locked in, locked out, locked up.

> LITTLE FAITH
> Locked together.

> FAITH
> Locked apart. A metaphor for what's to
> come. The end.

> LITTLE FAITH
> Through each other?

> FAITH
> The end to alter the way we remember
> the beginning. To terminate the middle.
> Engrave to forget. Forget to remember.

Numbers, initials, letters, names,
dates. Places, people, moments. Shared
and unshared.

                    LITTLE FAITH
A little act of faith.

                    FAITH
Read the scrawled Sharpie text: Drew
and Brenda. And, conjunction and
conjoining. The more elaborate the
display, the more expected the severing.
It's more than the picking of a lock.
You broke it. No, already broken.
Too red to remain untarnished. Too
bright to remain undiminished. Signs.
Declarations. Vows. Public displays
of affectation. Everlasting love,
hmm? I wonder how many per month the
Department of Transportation cuts off?
How do they choose? Does one lock look
more promising than another? Do they
read the inscriptions? Select the most
rusty-looking locks? Once cut, do they
discard? How many lonely staff members
cut and keep? A memento of a moment.
Quick, little Faith, define relationship.

                    LITTLE FAITH
"The way in which two or more concepts,
objects, or people are connected, or the
state of being connected."

                    FAITH
The *evanescent* way.

Little Faith recaptures the heart-shaped lock. She
holds it up like an exhibit.

                    LITTLE FAITH
Are you the mouse or the cat?

                    FAITH
Bu dong.

                    LITTLE FAITH
Xiao laoshu or *mao?*

                    FAITH
You tell me, wise little one. Whichever
one survives to tell tales.

                    LITTLE FAITH
You miss the point. *Yi zhi ban jie*, to
know one and understand half. Do you eat
the risk or watch and lurk?

                    FAITH
Both. You can do both.

                    LITTLE FAITH
Of course. But you do neither. You talk
down from Manhattan Tower. You point at
the people who try. Failures, successes,
no matter.

                    FAITH
Spare me.

                    LITTLE FAITH
You spare yourself. When's the last time
you chanced? When you revealed a feeling
to someone without knowing how that
person would react? You're a dilettante
of feelings. A dilettante emoter.

                    FAITH
You know nothing. How young are
you? Six? Eight? You shouldn't know
"dilettante." You shouldn't even know
"reveal."

                    LITTLE FAITH
I'm the little mouse within. I never
fear the fall, or what waits at the
bottom. The fall marries beauty and
pain. We haunt our hurts to the point of
forgetting our pleasures. We can choose.

                    FAITH
There's a rumble before the fall.
There's a loss before the landing.

Little Faith disrobes, folding her wedding garment on the bench. She removes her phoenix-crown headdress and sets it on Faith's lap.

                    LITTLE FAITH
          I'm going to swim among the keys.

Little Faith stands on the bridge's ledge and calls back to Faith.

                    LITTLE FAITH
          Jiligulu gun xialai.

Faith listens to the splash. She runs her fingers across the tops of the pearl-shaped baubles. She traces the wingtips of the phoenix decorations.

                    FAITH
          "Rumble," the mouse fell off the lamp.

ON THE CUFF

FAY

FADE IN:

**INT. WEST VILLAGE, NEW YORK - FAY'S 90-SQ-FT APT
- MORNING**

Hua takes off her stilettos and places them on the
shoe rack. She puts on house slippers and turns away,
but returns to align the heels so they're visually
parallel, toes and heels in line with each other.

> FAY (O.S.)
> You do everything so deliberately. With
> such deliberation.

> HUA
> *Sheng nu*, cut the reverence from your
> voice. It's a curse.

> FAY (O.S.)
> The deliberation, or the reverence?

> HUA
> You tell me.

> FAY (O.S.)
> But I asked you!

> HUA
> Sorry, I think the therapy's getting to
> me.

Hua pulls out a FOLDING CHAIR from between the shoe
rack and the wall. She unfolds it and sits on the edge,
hands laced on her lap.

> HUA
> You never told me to relax. I'm not
> looking at it, but I feel its eye. Does
> no one else say that?

                    FAY (O.S.)
I'd say "you tell me," but how can you
know? It varies.

                    HUA
It's just a lens. A non-sentient
machine. That records. Picks up sound
and sight. And yet. How unnerving. To
think about how you're seen, in that
clinical, mechanical way. Red light
blinking. Why does red mean record?
Surely that adds to the discomfort.

                    FAY (O.S.)
I have no idea. Good question. Green
means go, after all.

                    HUA
Red for danger. For the dangerous
possibilities in what could be recorded.
Evidence of all kinds. Camera obscura
turned lux.

Hua crosses her legs and a house slipper falls off. She
returns both feet to their slippers and the floor.

                    HUA
There's a phrase in law. "In camera,"
where "camera" means "chamber." As
in, "the judge assessed the claims in
camera"—in his or her private chambers,
public and press excluded.

                    FAY (O.S.)
No article?

                    HUA
No. Not "in a camera" or "in the
camera." Just "in camera."

Hua stands and patters over to the kitchen table. She
picks up Fay's Nikon DSLR.

                    FAY (O.S.)
Ayi, you obviously have every right to
that camera, but please…

                    HUA
No worries. If I broke it, I'd buy you a
new one.

                    FAY (O.S.)
That's generous and I believe you, but
it'd be a different camera. I grew with
this one. We learned together. Damn, I
need to get out more.

                    HUA
At first thought, the privacy of a camera
seems illogical. But inside the camera,
what a covered cave. A vault.

Hua removes the Nikon's lens cap. She presses a button
and the camera whirs awake.

                    HUA
So many mechanisms inside. All shielded
by layers of armor. How many secrets does
the mechanic keep? Underneath, inside, in
between. Hidden crevices. One fault, one
misalignment, and clear failure.

Hua takes a picture of Fay filming.

                    FAY (O.S.)
Recording the recording? Since when do
you know how to use a DSLR?

                    HUA
When you sent us those pictures of
Atlas in front of St. Patrick's, Phil
obsessed. I bought him one for his
birthday.

                    FAY (O.S.)
Three months ago? I've never seen it at
your place.

                    HUA
I seem to be the only constant he wants
in his life.

                    FAY (O.S.)
Want to—

                    HUA
There's a world beneath the plastic.
What's responsible for recording the
moments, the ones we call memories?

                    FAY (O.S.)
If you really want, I could google—

                    HUA
I like the idea. I like this unknowing.
The mystery behind the mechanism. Time
capsule. A moment, encapsulated. A
camera's honest.

                    FAY (O.S.)
A video camera's dishonest?

                    HUA
A camera steals a moment. Is only capable
of a snapshot. It says, "I shutter and
wink. You press me and I blink. I take
a picture." A camera's honest about its
limitations. It promises a moment and
delivers only that.

Hua zooms in to take a picture of the video camera.

                    HUA
But a video camera…the allure of uncut
footage. Time and space. Rolling in real
time. One-dimensional, but the illusion
of more. Everything, the promise of
everything. Record. Play. Rewind. Forward.
Pause. A video camera promises you a world.

                    FAY (O.S.)
A lie? Or a dream?

                    HUA
A broken promise.

Hua returns the camera to its case and sits down, again
on seat's edge.

                    HUA
We want so much to remember. It's the
details. We know the panorama. The

details change. We forget. We try,
we shut our eyes, play the relevant
music, eat the same foods, touch the
same fabrics. We try until we remember
falsehoods. Or we remember nothing and
think that's true, the nothing.

The video camera promises a flawless
memory. We play when we watch. A
game. We play with ourselves, our
recollections. We watch and say, "I know
what happens next." We clap our hands
and predict as the recording tells. We
say, "That's exactly how it happened."
Or, "Who filmed this? That's wrong!"

                    FAY (O.S.)
Better to hold a static photo?

                    HUA
Phil brought out our wedding tape. Dug
out the VHS machine. Played it. Gave a
commentary, too. As if I couldn't gather
my own data. He needed to narrate.
To list the names of every relative,
now dead or alive. To pause and say,
"I remember how you tripped a little
on your train. How I steadied you—
discreetly. You can almost miss it.
See, right there—stumble! And I give
you my arm. I right you." Play-by-play
narration.

                    FAY (O.S.)
To prove what?

                    HUA
The existence of once. Not his
intention. But that's my takeaway.

MUG STAINS

JIA

JIA: *Ni chifan le ma?*

(Pause.)

FAY: No.

JIA: I can talk quick.

FAY: I just returned from work.

JIA: Two weeks. Your phone die twice? No charger? Too busy with videos of past to maintain present relationship?

(Silence.)

JIA: You never ask how I am. Everything so forced with you. Like scrubbing stains?

FAY: Stains?

JIA: Mug stains. You use a mug. For coffee, tea, cocoa. The liquid sits, bathes mug's lining. No matter if you drink fast, if you swallow to burn your taste buds off. No matter if you steep soft and short. Lift your empty mug. Hold it to the light. Tell me what you see.

FAY: Stains?

JIA: Along the rim and rung around, spiraling down to the base. Deepest, darkest stains always coat the base, meeting point between bottom and circled corner.

FAY: Circumference.

JIA: Stop interrupting. Hope you have daughter just like you! You find the stain. Levels of stain. If you think straight, you fill mug to top and soak. You let sit. When you return, you examine again.

FAY: Time-consuming. Reexamine.

JIA: You reexamine, and—

FAY: Dishwasher?

JIA: *Zhu zui*! Your tongue flaps too much.

FAY: Sorry.

JIA: No apology, no words! Dishwasher. Still a *hai zi*? Always think of the easy way. Machine, use machine to work. For chores, for life skills. Devices never teach. Think. What, imagine your way? Machine magic, ah?

FAY: Saves human time and energy.

JIA: You think in the short. I say, think in the long. If you use machine magic, you become fooled gold. You run mug in the machine. But when you take dishes out—your problem: You expect machines to work for you—you find stains. Between, all along insides, lining, coating. What happened?

FAY: Weak dish detergent.

JIA: You think you fix next time. Use mug again and create new stains. New on top old. Swipe finger over stains. They stay; finger's unmarked. What now? You soak. And return to scrub what you missed first time. What the outcome? You wring sponge. You soap. You rub and water and swirl, and the stains laugh. They found home in your mug.

FAY: Accumulation.

JIA: Build, you build stains on stains. Fresh stains layer old ones. Now real hard fix, if any. May be too late. You scrub hard, sweating more than would-be first time. Hard, always fall for the hard way. You wait, hold off on attending to stains on the first find. What's that make you?

FAY: Lazy?

JIA: And stupid. I give you wisdom for free and you forever take me granted. Who can be me for you? Who taught you to run cold water over bloody cloth to stop setting of stains? Stain wants staying power. You feed it with your faults and flaws. Stop feeling entitlement. You must work, scrub your way to stay, to better. You want stains? No, just permanence. You want to become stain, not be *the* stain. Sustain yourself with work. No more "forgetting" to call. Pick up my calls. Pick up my voice messages. I leave messages for hearing. And next time, eat before I call.

KINESTHESIA

FAY

SHE ENTERS THE ROOM AND Fay knows without looking. Without needing to smell coconut hair products, to hear the absence of heel in her version of heel-toe walking, to recognize by the dagger-like scar two inches above the side of her left ankle, to remember the time they dared each other to eat a plateful of *hishi mochi* on Doll's Day—how their tongues burned with the sugar overdose.

Her every movement feels sensational. She stops in front of Fay and the latter knows the former. Knows beyond the usual five ways.

The weight of this awareness transmits to Fay's muscles and joints. As an arthritic woman kneads her knees and looks to the sky, she knows. The summer of her awareness ever lasts. The best part? Fay can never know this woman's mind. No amount of money in the world could open her head.

Fay listens to her. She listens, proprioceptors screaming. This best-everything woman stands before you. Position your awareness; attune your movement. Muscle and joint your way into her graces. Receive her receptors.

This level of consciousness grants highs and lows. She learns to think of another in a way that redefines the possibilities in connection. But such other-driven awareness also numbs her from her self.

She is the only nature Fay cares about. When they exercise at the gym, sweat droplets a summer necklace, Fay hears the grass, the roots, the ants, the breeze.

They share a pint of Neapolitan Ben & Jerry's, throwing more rainbow sprinkles at each other than in the carton. The grass, the roots, the ants, the breeze.

They read *The Book of the Thousand Nights and a Night* at the Strand, each teasing the other for smelling the loved pages. The grass, the roots, the ants, the breeze.

They watch *Inside Out* in the theater for the fourth time, picking wayward popcorn out of each other's hair. Grass, roots, ants, breeze.

Add such heightened attuned-ness to every conversation.

Fay: *Hearing the grass grow.* "Another glorious day at the press?"

She: "Today the editorial committee meeting took place, and we ordered too much food like usual."

Fay: *The roots shifting in the earth.* "Conference room drowning in vegan sandwiches?"

She: "Yes, and most left chunks on their plates. Like they're boycotting crumbs."

Fay: *The ants climbing up the blades.* "Which corner did you stop on this time?"

She: "Forty-Sixth and Park."

Fay: *The breeze tousling grass hair.* "George and his crew?"

She: "No; they left. New people in need."

Fay: *Grass roots ants breeze.* "You always were the bleeding heart."

WRITTEN IN THE FILES

HUA

"HOW MUCH INFORMATION ABOUT OTHERS do we gather, Dr. Morass? No need to furtively glance at your filing cabinet. I'm no thief.

"Think, though, of the data we collect—right or wrong. When I entered your office for the first time, you took inventory of me before I even opened my mouth.

"That may be, but I've nothing to lose by guessing the details of your report. 'Counseling intake form stated age forty-eight. Could pass for ten years younger. Appears adaptive aggressive. Walked in with minimal sound and weight, like she's afraid of being swallowed by the carpet. Subtle, inoffensive vanilla perfume. Simultaneously fills the room and shrinks into a corner.'

"I'm more self-aware than you think. When I'm here I may act like I'm in time-out, but we know why that's my initial reaction. Certain truths live in the unsaid, stuck in a fetal state. My family raised me to believe in destiny. Buddhism, reincarnation, karma. All ontologies to help us cope. My infertility's happenstance. But it'd be perfect if it were fate.

"My body's an inhospitable environment for growth because it's the lived expression of my mind. I know my problems exist. I choose to lie to myself. To smother into silence. I work in a field where reading about and meeting people who've lived through atrocities are guarantees. My marriage and my unclaimed self deserve less attention.

"You say that the problems of others never invalidate my own, and vice versa. And that comparison kills growth and joy. But think of your files, doctor.

"You shake your head, but I know you're thinking of them. The cases. Those copious notes. Diagnoses, events, names, relations, hang-ons, hang-ups. How soon after we leave this couch do we melt from people into studies?

"We think of you. This makes you uncomfortable. Yes, after hours, we replay our sessions. When you average five sentences per fifty-five-minute session, afterward we've no choice but to imagine.

"For better and worse, we're inside *your* head. Your mouth moved little, but your body shifted. Positioning, rustling, legs crossed, uncrossed, and crossed again. Each movement's a judgment. A thought borne out of a scratch, a cough.

"Surely you compare us. Too easy to avoid. Alphabetically there for your weighing. Perhaps you replace our names with our conditions. Psychological nicknaming. Bed-wetter, adulterer, egoist, coward, addict, liar, nymphomaniac, hermit.

"What happens when we fit more than one label? Do you resort to our names? Are our conditions stand-ins for our beings? Are we mannequins and our codes real? Stripped of our senses, we struggle to fight unknown burdens. Individuals against universals. Distinct against common. Write me in. Write me out. Write me down. What helps, what hurts, and what's the sense?"

INELUCTABLE LOSSES

Hua

HUA, PHIL, JIA, AND FAY stood around the bed like wingless, voiceless magpies.

"Ms. Wu, please print your name here, date here, sign here. We'll need two witnesses, please. Yes, just sign and print.

"Any limitations? I.e., restrictions to a complete postmortem examination. Permission granted for removal and retention as deemed appropriate by pathologists. Otherwise write none. It's all there in the bold print. We use organs, tissues, and fluids for research and education purposes. The clinical nurse will provide post-mortem care.

"No doubt—she's dead. We discourage use of euphemisms. No need to risk misinterpretations. Please discuss with the nurse administrator if you have further questions."

They voiced no questions. The original Ms. Wu lay before them, stiffening as they unspoke. Through the blind-drawn window beamed the edge of night. Hua shuffled to the window and opened it. The footsteps of people walking to, from, and by Methodist Hospital sounded like pounding gavels.

Heart attack leading to cardiac arrest. The latter malfunction the cause of amortization. *Amor* and *mort*. Love and death. Heart arrest. Arresting of the heart. A permanent rest. The hitherto unstoppable Ma Wu.

Hua wanted to remove the AED from the wall and defibrillate her mother. Ma hated being touched by strangers. Especially non-Chinese-speaking strangers. But if Hua administered the shocks, if she placed her hands on those still-ring-wearing fingers, whispering *wo hui lai le*—I am back—and then alternated between compressing Ma's chest and defibrillating, if Hua did all this there'd be no alternative than to shock her to life again. To feel Ma's hands flutter, hear her croak the same in response, *wo hui lai le*.

But the doctor recorded time of death. They were viewing her body for the last time. Ma Wu had ceased being. The doctor's words revisited. No doubt dead. No passing on, beyond, away. No veils. A simple seizing, seizure of the heart. Dead end, end zone. Exit only. Full stop. Death of a matriarch.

And at the root? Their fault. No. No mincing. Your fault. Completely preventable.

"You *chou biaozi*, stinking whore—"

A slap echoed. In the white room, it sounded black. Hua left the spinning in her head to look up.

Phil wound Jia's arms down to her sides. Fay touched her cheek and then glanced at her hand as if expecting blood.

Say something. You can right this. Now, before it worsens.

"Jia, neither the time nor…"

"Ma'am, I understand you're upset…"

"No daughter mine! How you *dare* stand there in pretend grieve, you murderer…"

"Ma'am, no one murdered anyone; while unexpected, the death…"

"They're upsetting other patients…"

"You need to leave. Please pay your last respects…"

Hua followed the group to the door, pausing at the threshold. The remaining nurse used Vaseline to slip off Ma's rings. Four jade; four gold. Hua cradled them in her palms.

"You can stay for a moment more."

Eight lucky rings in hand, Hua returned to Ma's bedside. Remembering the motherly gesture, she smoothed Ma's faint eyebrows, frown-line to temple. Hua opened her mouth to speak, and her voice emerged sounding like Fay's. The voice of Fay at age six, during Chinese homeschool lessons. Voice high and tight, but with quivering delivery.

Wo duibuqi ni. Ru guo wo shuo dui bu qi, ni shi fou jiu hui yuan liang wo?

I have wronged you. If I say I'm sorry, will you be able to forgive me?

DEAR DREW

JIA

THANKS TO YOUR CONCERN, I write to you now. I wanted to answer your calls, but strength failed me. I take time from work and spend it sleeping on my mother's clothes and then ironing them if I able to leave bed.

We never asked if she want cremated. As I type this, her urn sits beside me. No will or last tantamount. She never say any words about her mortality. I knew better not attempt that conversation.

There's much blame to list. That night I left Ma at Fay's to prepare for your visit. Visit that fell through, and daughter that fell through, too.

I question every step before that night. How many times I encourage death's company?

Week before, I moved a clock into the room Ma slept. Chinese superstition says clock gifts count seconds down to receiver's death. "To give a clock," *song zhong,* sounds like phrase meaning "to pay one's last respects." We were raised to see a clock and think "the end." But I here in America so long, I forgot. And so I forgot remedy, where money exchange transfers a purchase from giver to receiver. Or maybe Ma forgot, or pride stopped her from buying her clock.

I check the weather every morning, and that morning the forecast made for rain. When I packed her bag, I slipped in an umbrella. *San,* umbrella, and *san,* scatter or part (different tones) are another ominous pairing.

Yes, these are traditions and superstitions. America runs on money and logic. The Chinese and Taiwanese drive each other by fear and debt.

I thought Ma my burden. I gave her ill-fated gifts, cursing her. Now she'll return my accident favors. Ghosts hold a special role in our minds. Ma will come to collect my debts. In many Chinese stories, ghosts return to haunt families, but in disguise. Could be in person or in animal. On street corner or on bridge. Crossover, crossing…

But none of this happen if Fay be good. I can't tell you here, and in person is unimaginable. (Perhaps meeting would be mistake, and asking for more trouble?) I just say that she shamed us all, and that shame shocked Ma to death.

You'll write back to caution me. Mother already lose, but you can prevent losing your daughter out of anger. I deserve to cut her off. She dishonored us and Ma, especially because she refuses to own mistake. She repeats her claim that what Ma found wasn't hers, and that no one could've predicted the outcome. I refuse to raise a liar.

TETRAPHOBIA

JIA

JIA NOTED THAT THEY MADE a square. Four people, four chairs, four points, four perspectives.

Iterations of four littered her sister's apartment. Four tea towels. Four plants. Four bookshelves. Four large-scale framed pictures. Like Hua's begging for death. *Si*, four, and *si*, death. There's good reason to avoid fours. Momentarily, those four distinct voices intruded. Jia closed her eyes against the blackness and the threats faded. She forced herself to focus on the nightmare at hand.

She realized they were meeting four weeks after Ma's death. Chance or omen? They seemed to be waiting for her to speak.

"Yes?"

"What will we do with Ma's ashes?"

"Nothing."

Hua frowned. "You plan to keep them in the urn for decorative purposes?"

Anger swelled like a fresh injury. "Everything falls to me. Because I'm *jie jie*? Little sister, you want to skim your niece's stupidity? You handle. Or ask *that girl* to handle."

Her daughter leaned forward in her chair. "That girl?"

"More specific, ah? *Na ge lanbi.*"

"Jia! Respect your daughter."

"*Ayi*, what'd she call me? She never taught me that one."

Jia rose to pour herself more oolong tea. "A rotten cunt." She ignored Fay's stare.

"Interesting."

Phil cleared his throat. "Ladies, let's try to hold a civil dialogue."

They sat, each lost in their respective cup of oolong.

"No. I'm tired of letting the subtext live. Let's tear it out. Ma, say what you want. Give me your best."

Jia swallowed too quickly. She held back the coughs that clawed up her throat. "First, stop calling me that."

"What?"

"You're not my daughter. No more *nu er*. No more Fay. She died when she killed my mother."

"*Jie jie*, careful now—"

"Shut up, Hua. What you know about child-rearing? Know your place."

The pause that followed had time to birth silent children.

"Go on, then, Mrs. Wu Goodson. That a formal-enough breaking of relations? Why not renounce me four times to really kill it?"

Drinking more tea, Jia avoided the three sets of eyes. When she'd burned her tongue to numbness, the words emerged without a struggle.

"*Si buyaolian.*"

Faith laughed. The sound reminded her of the time the five-year-old girl scraped two kitchen graters together.

Jia felt more than saw Faith shirk Hua's touch. She felt Hua's pain, doubled.

"*Ci chu bu liu ren zi you liu ren chu.* Know that one, *shu shu* Phil? In this place I'm trash, but somewhere else I'll be a treasure."

"Fay, you know she—"

"She means what she says. Speak now, Mrs. Wu Goodson, or we'll assume you're still the 'woman of the word' you raised me as. Listen to the nothingness. Feel the weight of finality. She wants to speak her mind? Fine. I will too."

Jia felt an unknown, unnamed bond snap.

"My turn to dole out some long-spun truths. Hold your nose, Mrs. Wu Goodson, because this'll smell *and* taste funny."

Her bile spread. Jia felt it overtake her palate, stream up her nasal cavity, and run down her throat, squeezing the elements in her chest.

Faith rose, hands together behind her back, like in her childhood Chinese-speech competition days.

Jia blinked away the bile from her eyes.

"I'm bi. The 'B' in LGBTQIA+. Bisexual. Some prefer pansexual because of gender nonconforming and trans people. I like the sound of 'bi' better and believe it can encompass my ability to find anyone attractive. Bi to me means dueling and accepting dualities within myself. Now let me be clear: None of us wanted *Lao lao's* death. Especially the suddenness of it. I called 911 and you immediately. But no one arrived prepared—for her death, for the shock.

"I'm bi, but I'm not responsible for my grandmother dying. And as I told you before, those weren't my magazines. I didn't, neither directly nor indirectly, give her a heart attack, and lead her to cardiac arrest. The EMT pried *someone else's* magazine from her fists. Not to get graphic, but I know what's mine, and I know my style. I knew *lao lao* would be visiting. I'd never leave anything potentially explosive around for her to find. You think I underestimate an old Taiwanese woman? She'd slept over before. Without fail, I'd wake the next day to find some of my belongings...shifted. She liked to snoop. She held no respect for even the idea of privacy.

"I refuse to retract my position. Who knows how those magazines arrived at my apartment? I didn't knowingly accept or store them. *Lao lao* saw them for the first time, and then I saw them for my first time.

"But who cares? Why's it matter anymore? All I know is I'm no longer going to live a lie. I'm sorry *lao lao* died, and in such a way. But yes, Mrs. Wu Goodson, *si buyaolian*. When I die, I hope to go without shame. Love or leave accordingly."

Faith returned to her seat, chair ends jarring against the floor.

For a moment, no one moved. Then something cut through the air, slammed against the refrigerator, and fell, taking a paper casualty with it. They registered the crash before connecting the whizzing object to it. They assessed the aftermath. At the refrigerator's feet were a shattered saucer and Phil and Hua's food expiration list. Hua stood by the saucer's remains, unrepentant.

"How dare you. How dare you use your grandmother's death as a self-righteous coming-out opportunity. If shameless is what you're going for, you're off to an early start."

The tone rather than the words drew Jia's attention to her sister's voice. Hua's prowling-tiger prosecution tenor. Hua sat back down but seemed straighter than the chair holding her up.

"Shut your mouth, Phil, unless you want to welcome a nest of fruit flies. I have self-control. I'll forgo invoking expletives. Young woman, you're twenty-five. Did we raise you to be this solipsistic, this sanctimonious? What do you know of the world, let alone your place in it? I'm disappointed you've chosen this moment, when we're discussing the state of this already-broken family, to wave your experimental *freak* flag in our faces. I should be accustomed by now, but the selfishness of your generation continually astounds me."

Faith's sobs were quiet. Apologetic in emanation. Jia sat on her hands, feeling the buttons on her jean pockets begin imprinting on her skin. The tangible sensation grounded her.

"You know Jia and I took *lao lao* in despite many obstacles, including—but not limited to—feelings and circumstances. A crisis calls for unification. Who cares if they're your motherfucking magazines or not? We're left with a dead mother, one we'd spent decades away from. She died in an undignified manner, and you bragging about your alternative lifestyle pays ill tribute to her existence and memory. Where is your sense of time and place? Disgraceful. You sound like a millennial white feminist bitch. That who you aspire to be when you look in the mirror?"

"Hua—"

"I'm not finished, Phil. As children, when we did wrong, we used to kowtow—"

Jia compressed her bottom against the backs of her hands, feeling greater pressure.

"Hua! *Enough*."

Faith's backpack whispered its goodbye to the floor. The door to the condo apologized its way closed.

The room was deadly silent without Faith's sobs.

"What the fuck, Hua? She's our niece! You were supposed to diffuse. Instead, you escalate? Where's your head at?"

"I—I…don't know. I'm sick of everything. It just boiled over."

"Fucking hell."

As Hua slumped against her chair, Jia dragged her hands free. A circular printed message outlined her weary skin. One for each jean button; one for each hand. Four words: MADE IN THE USA.

CHOOSE BETWEEN BRUSHING
AND FLOSSING

FAY

ON THE SCREEN, *THE JOY LUCK CLUB* began. A single white feather floated down to rest on a black ground. Fay sat on her bed, folding laundry, while Summer checked on the stove.

"Smells like we've got some burn-outs."

Summer snapped the stove dial to zero. "Too high a flame, apparently."

"How burnt?"

"Toasted. You'll eat them."

Fay rolled off the bed, folded clothes in her arms. "Presumptuous. We should be eating crab. Of the best quality."

"We haven't reached that scene yet. No jumping ahead." Summer nodded at Fay's dresser. "Want to file and then help me season?"

They worked without speaking, half-listening to the Asian mothers in the film bicker over mahjong. Fay reached over Summer's head, covering the cabinet's edge with her palm, to peruse her spice rack.

"It's not going to hit me. I'm too short, remember?"

"Safe habits."

While Summer separated the burnt from the unburnt popcorn, Fay scooped black pepper, garlic powder, paprika, and ground ginger into a metal bowl.

"Ready to season it? I've got the parmesan, too."

The pair mixed together, lifting and overturning the puffs, the few un-popped kernels protesting against the bowl in a clanging fashion.

Summer brought the popcorn to the foldout coffee table, the distinct spices wafting together.

"I used to resent that they didn't cast the Hapa character with a Hapa actress. Now I'm glad. How often do Asian actors work?"

"About as often as our Asian parents hug us."

They folded Fay's bed into couch form. Their wrists skimmed when they sat down in front of the television.

Summer moved forward. "Mom used to hug me often."

Fay moved backward, curling against the armrest. "Italians love amore."

"Asians too, in their own way."

"Straight-up A's. Play the piano. Win your chess competitions. Make a name to ring in church like wedding bells."

Summer tossed popcorn down Fay's shirt. "Their love lives in the unsaid."

"Unhurt me, then."

"I—it's the rape scene. Fay, have mercy; throw me the remote or mute it. I hate hearing her struggle."

"You'd rather she take it silently?"

"What? It's like you want a root canal. For your heart."

Fay smiled. "Appropriate metaphor, considering that I went to the new dentist this morning. I doubt that my insurance covers that procedure, though."

"You made the switch? Still unsure what for. How often would you expect to meet them there?"

"For preventative purposes. Who knows how long this'll last? I bet Dr. Chung would tell Ma about my upcoming appointments. She could plan an ambush. I want to avoid run-ins. I hate scenes."

Summer unmuted the film. "Scenes you can't direct, you mean."

"Apparently I've been flossing wrong all this time."

"You'd rather play chess than perform. Strategy over art. Yet you're the most creative person I know. How is that?"

At Summer's signal, Fay muted the film again. They respectfully waited for the young woman onscreen to finish wailing over her drowned baby.

"The hygienist said that I should floss first, and end with brushing. That I need to floss up and down—three times—between each tooth, on each side. 'Contrary to popular belief, brushing comes last. What's brushing? Surface cleaning; polishing. Flossing—that's the real work.

Between the crevices. If you're forced to choose, floss instead of brush.'
I suppose we need to privilege invasive investigation."

Fay handed Summer a tissue.

"Gets me every time. And what miserable advice! I hate flossing."

"Enjoyment or toleration plays no role here."

Sliding over, Summer rested her head on Fay's lap, shifting to better
see the television.

"You're killing me. Now where do I place my popcorn?"

"Leave it? You're down to the real burn-outs anyway. We're approaching the salon scene. More tissues! Stroke my hair?"

"I'd need to wash my hands first, unless you want spices everywhere."

"Napkins."

As Summer further settled onto Fay's lap, the latter relinquished
her hopes for separation. Suppressing a sigh, Fay wiped her hands and
did what she wanted.

"Flossing always hurts. Either it's uncomfortable, or you bleed.
Three times per side? Who wants to attack gums like that?"

"Necessary for long-term health. To prevent teeth from falling out.
We need to chew. We hope to chew with the teeth we grew."

Roots to tips, Fay flossed her best friend's hair. Softer than memory,
and more malleable, too. Even with her face a foot away, she could
smell the coconut products.

"I love when you finger through my strands. Better than any brush."

"I bet."

"What?"

"I pet."

"Right. This is what flossing should feel like. Soothing. Safe. I could
fall asleep to this. That's what missing from every failed relationship.
Argue about duties and money, but really the problem's a lack of trust.
Miscommunication. Are your hands tired? Theodore complained after
three minutes of this."

"No. Ah, so that's why you broke up with him! The Asian nicknames
were okay, but the lazy hair petting..."

"China doll, you so funny."

"Whatever, Japanese rose. Little geisha girl."

"Massage my hair, Lucy Liu!"

Fay resumed flossing, resigned. She'd threaded herself into this situation.

Summer threw popcorn at the antagonistic husband onscreen.

"Sorry; I'll clean later. But there's my point. They built that relationship on brushing. Look at how white the surface is. No one seeks the debris between."

Fay tousled Summer's bob. "Now you love flossing? Because I'm in your hair?"

"No. I still hate flossing. A painful process. But I believe in its importance."

They returned to the film for a few scenes, sometimes saying lines before the actors began them.

"No offense, as I love this scene," Fay said, "but no one possesses a best-quality heart."

"Pessimist."

"Realist."

"Realistic pessimist. You understand necessity, but you expect flossing to hurt."

Fay blew Summer's bangs off her forehead.

"We struggle between fictions, large and small. World and country. Country and state. State and town. Town and community. Community and friends. Friends and family. Family and partners. Partners and children. Children and self. Whom do we connect with? Who's capable of connection?"

On the television, the first-time-meeting sisters hugged against the backdrop of a passenger ship.

Summer reached for another tissue. "The end always makes me cry. But who says we need to choose between brushing and flossing?"

"Others. But even if we overthrow them, we ask ourselves the same. Invasive investigation's exhausting. Connecting's hard. Flossing hurts. Sometimes we know the full truth, but we choose the half-made one."

THE UNCOOKED CENTER

HUA

THE SCIENCE OF BAKING SEEMED senseless to Hua. Confined by fixed measurements but complicated by words like "pinch" and "dash."

He wanted her to bake. He wanted *them* to bake. Alongside ten other couples. A different iteration of school, of class, of learning.

"It's time you overcame your fear of cake," Phil joked, flicking a lump of flour toward her. It hit her wrist and burst into separate particles of powder, dusting her jade bracelet.

"How much did you pay for this course?"

"You should take that off."

"No thanks."

"You don't need to wear your mother's bracelet *all* the time."

She stopped herself from drinking in the bruise on his temple. From her wrist to his head. If only she embodied the power of jade.

When the instructor came by, Hua feigned interest in the "tips and tricks." Then she returned to cracking eggs. Phil beat them with the electric mixer while Hua added the granulated sugar. They mixed and added, Phil insisting on Hua handling the red food coloring.

As he spooned the pre-refrigerated ganache into ramekins, Hua dropped the red-velvet mixture over his work. She decided that she found Phil tolerable when silent.

"Chill, heat, and then eat," she read from the whiteboard.

"When's your next session with Dr. Morass?"

Hua sat on the edge of her stool and shrugged.

"I noticed you skipped for the past two weeks. Why?"

"Needed a break from all the listening."

Phil sat next to her. "Maybe I should join. Couples therapy."

"I'm going to peek at our dish. You know what they say. Edges are the first defined, the first heated, the first to burn; the center remains uncooked the longest."

"Who says that?"

She took the lava cakes out a couple seconds before the oven timer beeped. The small rebellion felt like lifting her spine.

Phil handed Hua the camera she'd bought for him. Following his implicit directions, she took pictures.

"I want my friends to almost taste the molten chocolate. To feel the stickiness of the cake on their fingertips."

When they could loosen the cakes' edges, Phil plated them.

"Did you poison them?"

"What?"

Phil poked her thigh with the prongs of his fork. "At least try one."

He piled extra whipped cream on top of her lava cake. Digging far beneath the cream, Hua excavated a quarter-sized piece out. She chewed it. When finished, she resisted the temptation to open her mouth like she did at the dentist's.

"Told you this would be a great idea. Admit it."

"You're right."

As soon as she said the words, Phil left their station to network. He left some of his business cards at their table in case someone decided to talk to Hua.

Phil Ting, Distinguished Professor of Law. Ting, like *ting*, listen, or obey. *Bu ting*, incessant. *Ting zhi bu qian*, stagnant.

Against his velvet chuckle, against the laughter he induced in the other couples, she created a mental list. All alternative meanings involving his surname.

Ting bu dao. Can't hear.

Ting er bu wen. Deliberately ignore.

Bu ting ming. Disobey.

Ting bu. Come to a stand.

Bai ting bu yan. Worth hearing one hundred times.

Bu wen jiu ting bu dao jia hua. Don't ask and you'll be told no lies.

The scent of cream and chocolate sickened her. Without touching, she could feel the heavy, sweet combination stick her palms together. Sugar under her nails. Ganache between the webs of her fingers. Flour coating the tops of her nails like ghost markings.

She tasted raw eggs in her throat. Thick yolk, thin but cohesive egg whites. Bits of shells cutting into her throat. Steadying her hands, she downed her cup of water. The feelings loosened by a margin.

The business cards beckoned her periphery. Hua wanted to snip them into confetti. Instead, she returned to her lava cake. Selecting his fork, she pressed from one side of the cake into the center. The weakest point. Cream fell into ganache, and ganache oozed the red velvet apart. Chocolate and blood. Sweet heart.

AFTERWARDSNESS

HUA

HUA SAT IN HER BATHTUB, skin wrinkled the point of peeling. Wrinkled, but not to the point of completion. She relit her vanilla-lavender candle and waited for the scent to rekindle.

With nothing yet wafting in her direction, she entered another mind warp.

She thought of many complaints but overturned the justification of each one's individual existence. Collectively, she denied herself permission to complain.

What rights did she hold, anyway? Beyond statehood and contracts. What about capitalization permissions? Pronoun rights? The first-person singular? What right did "I" hold to capitalization? Lowercase, uppercase, why? Who did "I" claim to be? A VIP according to whom?

Freud to Lacan, Lacan to Laplanche, and all the scholars before, during, and after; remembered, forgotten, and unknown. If babies swam out of the womb unsuspecting and incognizant, at what point did that shift?

Unable to remember. She wanted to remember the time before self-consciousness. Before, when she was unable to walk and a hand placed her before a mirror and pointed. You, on the other side. Hear that gurgle? You, your voice. Your palms together—your clap. Holding your own hands.

Turn it on yourself. Speaker of your own sentences. Your favorite subject. Say ah, eye, I. At the center of your pupil.

Are you feeling yourself, your selves? Which of you claims I? Step out from the otherness. Write out of misrecognition, unrecognition. You became your own alien. Only you can marry your separations.

HUNGER MANAGEMENT

JIA

WITHOUT HUA, I WOULD OWN no Fay documenting. Today means one month from her outburst at that family meeting.

To the world, I profess ownership of no daughter. No *xin xin*, no Fay, no Faith. Without child and childless. Life without complication. By my self.

But after talking over the phone with Drew, hearing him spew about Harmony and Will, I feel the tapping fingers of regret. And when I return from massaging skin of strangers, weakness rises. I reach for my phone, for the speed dial I can't make to delete yet, and force my hands to drop. When urge hits again, I sit on the weakest part of my couch—middle, where little Fay jumped up and down till breaking a hidden structure. I sit on my hands, pressing my pants into hands' backs.

I let the Sina images flash over me. When the outside city lights fail me, I shake the four intruders in my head, tucking them under other memories. I turn all my lights on, electric bill damned.

Upset, angered, and bored with the state of Taiwan, I feed my television VHS of Fay. First sitting, first walking, first speaking. All of me to her: Mom and Ma and *Niang*.

On the radio I heard a woman say mothers and fathers grieve for children differently. Moms cry for child and memories of her. Dads cry—when alone and unwatched, I think—for grown-up they imagined child to become.

I steep in it all. I am at once tea leaves and boiled water. I scorch myself till I ink out, tainting the water. Unfurl in drops.

When I play Fay tapes, I avoid watching. Sometimes I catch reverse reflections from my framed pictures, but I turn my head, avoiding a stare.

Even without looking, I know what happens. Easy when most filmed moments involve food. For me, always feeding. For Hua, always teaching. The nannies in Taiwan and the cooks and maids taught me home training. Between me and the professor, I made an adult child.

Her laughs never happen in my tapes, only in Hua's. In mine, you can hear her formal address even when she's silent. Especially when silent. Whether in child jeans, nylon pants, or silk, she glided. She would make principal ribbon dancer. Used to. Once.

Every Saturday morning, seven a.m., I took her without holding hands—I taught her to need and want leaning on no one—to the Taiwanese open market. Without perfection, but good enough. Walking between stalls, I let myself forget I landed in America, struggling to outrun NYC teeth.

Our own Fruit Kingdom. The vendors replicated Taiwanese dirt too well, but fruit varieties made the worth. I would pick star fruit, feeling, pressing, pushing into skin, massaging for depth and promise, and she observed. Then she picked, and we compared. And green mangoes, Buddha's Heads, guavas, dragon fruits, loquats, muskmelons, pomelos, longans, jujubes, sugar canes. Two of each; one from me, one from her.

And my proudest moment, teaching her to accept durian. I would choose the biggest, spikiest, royalist of the pile and make her carry home in its own bag.

"Ma, *e chou pu bi*, the stench assaults the nostrils! Like down-stair *Ayi*, Auntie's garbage bin. Like *ye chou*, underarm stink."

You grow to love the smell. Strong and proud.

"Ma, like *chou dou fu*, stinky tofu?"

Yes. A rough outside, but silky inside.

She stopped complaining and would hold the bag open on the walk home. It spread like invisible octopus legs through our ninety square feet. Even after the cutting, eating, cleaning, and disposal, it suctioned to our walls.

With chicken feet, fish eyes, and pig's blood cake, the same. She trusted my taste. Trained her taste buds to orient to me. Accepted my judgments with no question.

She listened so good I hardly needed to hit her. From the time she stopped kicking in my belly, that night in my first Chinatown apartment when they woke us in midnight with black layers and flashing eye whites, teeth, she knew time and place and needed behavior by intuition.

I think that night she learned to listen. Because on my hospital bed, sweat bleeding from pores I never knew existed, she rolled out of me with little effort, with poke instead of push. A mew, a cough, and a quiet.

Without Hua here to judge me, I replay her tapes over mine. I listen to Fay sing nursery songs of Hua's childhood. Mandarin first, English second. Order of operation. Little Fay laughs in bursts, like sun appearing between summer showers. But careful. A pregnancy in her outbursts, a holding back of volume and force.

I now know. She hid from me then, too. Continual covering. The night my innocence died, hers died too. That normal part of her mutated. Twisted in my womb. Fetus Fay. She heard blunt movements, hair pulling, forcing down and up from my knees, wetness from me streaking against the wall in diagonal streams.

She understands without knowing. I feed her then, too. Before the born date, the cocooning out into air colder than gun metal, her skin absorbed my placenta fear. She ate my shame and drank my terror. And now she manages her hunger in this way. Thinks that the gentle sex makes up for the violent one. If I tell her, will she change? Will she hold my truth in an open bag, like once, waiting to adjust to stench, and eat fruit until it tastes without rot?

IT TAKES TWO TO TANGLE

JIA

internecine |ˌin(t)ərˈneˌsēnin(t)ərˈnēsīn|
adjective
destructive to both sides in a conflict.
ORIGIN mid 17th cent. (in the sense "deadly,
characterized by great slaughter"): from Latin
internecinus, based on *inter-* "among" + *necare* "to kill."

When my ex-daughter returned from her first semester at Barnard, I felt her changed. Cracks form over time. Womb to air. Fetus to female. Either too much yin, or too much yang in those drinking games. She thought I suspect nothing.

Drinks, drugs, sex: at parties, in books and music and TV. I thought about telling her about Drew and her first beginning. I thought to demand she live home. Hua and Phil and their lawyer-forked tongues, dipped in crystalized honey. Raised so well, knowing better, above true damage. Experiment in the short to reject in the long. First adult steps.

I misstepped. Missed needed steps. But where does an ordinary circle begin, one without yin or yang? Just white, blank, empty. So I listened, my first and last time, to voices of others. More intelligent and cultured, I thought. Voices drenched with power of western conviction. Voices like puffed chests. Let American live in America. Roots aside, depths ignored.

Fay returned on fairy wings. Moved like wisps of mist. Now you feel my particles, now I leave. Every piece of her seem lighter but stronger. More free but more exact. Intention-less but with intent.

She corrected me without pause. English first, then Mandarin. "Not 'intensive purposes.' Instead, 'all intents and purposes.' *Shi zhi shang.*

And before I forget, not 'underlining,' but 'underlying.' *Ji chu.* Say it after me? Ma, why are you crying? *Bu yao ku.* You know that saying Aunt Hua taught me, the other mountain's stone can polish jade. *Ta shan zhi shi ke yi gong yu.* Improve yourself by accepting criticism from the outside. This is easier—I'm on the inside. Aunt Hua, *Ayi* taught me. You did? I guess I remember differently. Here's the tissue box. I hate being watched when I'm upset; I think I get that from you. Call me when you need me. I'll be at the indie bookstore four blocks down—they're doing a spoken-word showcase tonight."

Two to tango sounds senseless. Two to tangle. Because instigator starts humiliation, and endurer feels consequences in mind, gut, and heart. Instigator spins thread, twisting, weaving string under, inside string; faster than the most winning ribbon dance, than the most accomplished yo-yo-ist. Into tangles, dragging sufferer inside net without beginning or end. No dance, no give and take. Taker and taken. The depleted. And yet, at core of the ball, tangled together in mutual destruction.

Spring rolls for the new year, her new freshman semester. My first batch in six years. Rolls lined on tray, between soggy and burnt, balanced on crisp. I felt my pride rise like the front end of lion dancers.

Americans sing about joys of surprise. Excitement of gifts, grown by unasked, unwanted, unknown. Open presents in front of giver. So giver can see receiver's face. What for? To lose it? Who acts that way?

I protected my spring rolls in a presentation case, glass lid. And I took a cab—a *cab*—to save my art from salivation of strangers on public transport. Spending without thrift for my only child, this daughter, this dean's list, this first-semester 4.0 honor. Expected, unspoken demands met, even in faces of temptation.

Three flights of stairs, no elevator. I paused on last landing to even my breaths. Odd, door left jarred. I thought she meant that, a welcome for me. Knee door middle to make my entrance. And that *la la yang guizi* lesby devil foreigner on not-my daughter. For how long? Rolling and rocking? Seeming with clothes, but no matter. Intent clearer than dirt on sun.

My fingers itched to fold, to let tray and glass fall to break to shard and dust. But I held on. I combed her eyes for excuse or explanation, for sorry. Instead, defiance in fire form. No thought of wrong, or wanting any insight from me. Rejecting nineteen years of me.

With grace, I set spring rolls down, smell of fresh vegetables and oyster sauce and handmade, hand-loved paper-thick wrappers bouncing with flavor so revolting I know my childhood favorite died here. At home my three imperfect batches will jump to *Ayi* Gui's kitchen table. This fourth batch can rot, waste damned.

She called an hour after. I heard the ring. Seven before the machine. Automate message, person you're calling is unavailable, please leave message after tone. "Mom." She cleared her throat once, twice. And hung up with faded slowness. I separated plug from socket, and red light stopped beating.

Every Saturday morning, when she knew I returned from street-vendor shopping, she called. Always that one American word, never Ma. Two, three beats, and hang up.

Hua called and I said Fay humiliated me in front of her roommate. She slipped into lawyer voice, but I stood my place. Second term ended, and we agreed Fay would stay at her condo, paying for space.

What happened, Hua asked time and again. Neither of you will tell me.

That second college year, I heard echoes of silence like lone bat in a cave. I called Hua during her office hours. How did Fay seem? Act? Sound? No more weight lost? How much of plate wasted? I demanded no interpreter, no mediation, no methods.

What am I supposed to do, Hua asked, record our dinner conversations? No. A joke! That's illegal. Sister or not, no.

But that summer before her third year, I returned from work, finding lemon-ginger tea waiting for me, a bowl of *ta-a* noodles, and her luggage in the closet.

Every time she sat with me, I waited for a never-arriving sorry. I spoke my Chinglish with purpose. And for rest of her stays on college breaks, she only responded in English.

I blocked the images, rolling of vegetables and meat into wrappers, vision of sameness together on dorm floor like stray dogs.

From where? Not from my side. I still feel weight of the tray, crinkle of parchment sheet. And sound of meeting, fumbling lips, clicking teeth. I block it all.

FUCK YOUR PLATITUDES

FAY

INT. SOUND STUDIO ON NINTH AVENUE, CONTROL ROOM - NIGHT

We hear microphone static. Long shot of CONTROL ROOM.
Static stops and silence beats.

> SANDSTORM
> These your digs?

> FAY (O.S.)
> No way. My former mentor's.

> SANDSTORM
> Lucky to have such connections. How
> big's your network?

> FAY (O.S.)
> Take me out to dinner first.

> SANDSTORM
> Ha! Divas do the dining.

> FAY (O.S.)
> Let's start there. Journey to becoming a
> diva.

Sandstorm adjusts her metallic-gold HIJAB. Under a
black corset, she sports a red long-sleeved shirt.

> SANDSTORM
> Sleepy-town start in the Midwest. Dad
> emigrated from Egypt to Wichita for an
> AuD degree. Sorry, Doctor of Audiology
> program. And before you ask, Kansas
> because his cousin lived there. Mom's
> also Egyptian, but second generation.
> She worked for the public library. He
> attended a technology-training class—
> think large computers—and a year later,
> post-ring-on-it moment, my brother
> graced the world with his presence.

                    FAY (O.S.)
How many years since you've been home?

                    SANDSTORM
(Clicking her tongue) Girl, I took the
"re" out of return when I left. Honestly.
They probably banned me from every flight
zone, highway, and bus station.

                    FAY (O.S.)

Rewinding, though, did you find a
commiseration with your brother? How
much older?

                    SANDSTORM
Two years. He's in Cali working for a
tech firm. In high school we bonded over
Eminem and made a pact to flip Wichita
the bird.

Sandstorm waves her MIDDLE FINGERS at the camera.

                    SANDSTORM
No disrespect to the city itself. Sucky
people live everywhere. Maybe I would've
felt drowned by air in Boston or Chicago,
too. But I didn't fit Wichita. Hit with one
too many epithets. It used to surprise
me, how creative closeminded people can
be. But then you realize: They hold
nothing but hate. If you make prejudice
your passion, hell yeah you'll dominate.

                    FAY (O.S.)
So you found solace in rap music and
Black culture?

                    SANDSTORM
You documentarian. Too neat a
transition. I ate dirt for a while.
Bullying of different shades. First
the tom girl with the too-brown skin.
Then at age twelve, an escalation of
difference because I began wearing a
hijab. I told my peers about Ramadan.
After the Towers, too, so I knew no one

appreciated my refusal to melt. The one
arena I tried to connect with lunch-
table queens? Usual pop artists—whiter
than vanilla.

> FAY (O.S.)
> You tell your parents about your
> troubles? Compare wounds with your
> brother?

> SANDSTORM
> My parents are bookish conservatives.
> Non-hypocritical Muslims. Praise Allah
> and be grateful. Feeling negative? Pray
> it away. Depressed? Ungrateful. You know
> how many jobs your father worked? How
> many connections he left in Egypt? The
> guilt and shame he feels for his current
> privilege? Imperfections are part of
> beauty. Think of Marilyn and her mole.
> Endearing. You can choose not to fit
> here. That's an honor.

> FAY (O.S.)
> I feel that.

> SANDSTORM
> Anyway, so I trudge through Wichita State
> as an accounting major. They let me minor
> in music theory and composition—best
> worst decision my parents made. Because I
> learned that the world I craved existed.
> That's when I discovered The Miseducation
> of Lauryn Hill.

> FAY (O.S.)
> But you stayed in Wichita?

> SANDSTORM
> An accounting firm recruited me. Stable,
> impressive income for a woman emerging
> with a bachelor's. Full benefits,
> walkable from my parents' house, and a
> known name. People piss on rappers and
> celebrities for perpetuating consumerism
> and materialism, but everyone except the

homeless folks on the street endorses
and partakes in superficial shit.

                FAY (O.S.)
Did you create on the side?

                SANDSTORM
Unofficially. I thought, who's this
whitewashed Brown chick, never missing
a prayer, living at home, waiting for
a man to marry for deliverance? The
game played me so well I became a cog.
And any time I complained to one of
my few friends, all they offered were
motivational posters.

                FAY (O.S.)
Literally?

                SANDSTORM
No, I mean they tried to shut me up
with clichés. Light after the tunnel. A
passing phase. You'll acclimate. Life.
Someone's got it worse. Beyond the brick
wall awaits glory.

                FAY (O.S.)
I'm unfamiliar with that last one.

                SANDSTORM
I improvised. But easily imaginable,
I think, given how often brick walls
appear in metaphors.

Sandstorm rises, stretching, showcasing COMBAT BOOTS
beneath her tiered red and black skirt.

                FAY (O.S.)
Want to explain your outfit?

                SANDSTORM
Despite my intolerance for girly girls,
I earned my A's in home economics. This
is a belly dance skirt; I took lessons
as a kid. Handcrafted, or "bespoke," as
they say in Europe. I know you mentioned
growing up with a couple Muslim friends,

but I recognize that a doc's a video
soapbox. May I?

I wear a hijab because I choose to. I
feel liberated because fewer men have the
balls to ogle me. My parents raised me
with certain beliefs, some of which I've
broken from. But I believe in my morals,
and I've cultivated a code I choose to
stick to—unlike flies to trap paper.

No one's forcing me—neither implicitly
nor explicitly—to do shit. I'm a grown-
ass woman. A badass bitch who happens
to go to the mosque and fast during
holidays and cover myself in a way that
opposes bare-all pop culture.

People tend to understand the covering
of skin but find hair shade the problem.
Listen: My hair's glorious. I know
this. My ladies know my truth. One day
the right guy—should he exist, although
I'll still diva on my own—will know. My
beauty, conventional or unconventional,
isn't for your consumption.

For some Muslims, I'm an infidel. Raisin-
picker, platitude-fucker, corset-wearer.
Dislike my art? Stop listening. Dislike
me? Impossible—you don't know me. And I
avoid assholes who erase space.

> FAY (O.S.)
Some advice for young women questing for
space in the world?

> SANDSTORM
Identify as you damn well please. Leave
yourself time to explore who you were,
are, and want to become. And then claim
self-made strength, and either flick off
or subvert the people and circumstances
that blockade your path. Hustle to
divadom, and then rock that diadem.

TISSUE FOR A TOURNIQUET

HUA

SHE UNLOCKS THE CONDO DOOR and listens with her fingertips. Smells for traces of poached eggs and burnt toast. But there's only the hint, like a breath, of last night's wine. Her skinny-heeled boots foray into the hallway. The wedding photos hiss from the wall, but they bounce off her like pebbles against an open umbrella.

Silence means safety. She turns the deadbolt and draws the chain. Can you call a place home if it's not a refuge? When does a layover become a lay?

Without his hands in the way, she brews coffee to her taste. Strong before, during, and after. Thorough and throughout. She reaches into the back of the cupboard for her cracked brown mug. Cracked at the lip, and in need of balm. Brown, he'd said, like dried blood. Why'd she want to drink out of dried blood?

She drinks her bitterness, cracked-mug lip against her own, daring a cut to happen. Challenge unaccepted, she rests her free hand against the marble countertop. She moves her thumb away from her fingers, pulling at the skin between. The scar awakens, stretching, and she remembers.

What are the tenets of toxic masculinity? The biggest no-no's, especially woman to man? Laugh at him. Tell him he's wrong. Blame him. What handle holds this fan together? The act of humiliation.

When one is unaware of what to duck, the preventables hit all targets.

In this kitchen, slicing red onions, the only kind he ate. A hug from behind, a slip, a gash. Streaming red, cover of blood so thick they couldn't see the problem. And then the reveal, the opening, the—

"Your thumb! Hanging by a...*fuck* by a—"

Scent of onion juice mixed with metallic warning.

He handed her a tissue and told her to wrap it. Too much visceral fluid. He took 911 into the other room.

"The emergency? Blood everywhere. Yes. A tissue. The first absorber on hand! No. Hua, you conscious? I never said 'scared.' It's not a phobia. I prefer to avoid it. Who likes it? Yes, pull up in front."

She snaked down to the floor, pressed her cheekbones against the ceramic tiles. Calming against her flushed cheeks. As she lay there, listening for the wail, blood leaking, she felt for the tissue.

The tissue had tried. Worked itself into nonexistence, into soggy remnants on her disconnected skin. She peeked and found the origin of the peculiar feeling: scraps lost in the rending of flesh and muscle. Would they extract, diving with tweezers for the Kleenex? What if they never found it; left it swimming beneath scar tissue?

In the ambulance, he held a tissue to his nose. Blood, he said, smelled like gun-metal. Slick iron.

At the hospital, his answer indicated his right to stay, but she asked him to wait outside, ignoring the nurse's brows, curved upward into question marks.

Excretions disturb him, she explained, as he hovered in the doorway, one foot on either side of the threshold.

Weak stomach? the nurse asked, injecting the last dose of local anesthesia.

She laughed, already feeling the limpness take hold. Husband: heart of a jellyfish.

These bits of…tissue? Who puts a *tissue* on an avulsion?

Ask him.

They listened to his footsteps clip the transition strip dividing the door from the hallway.

But through the soles of his feet, he heard the nurse: Did you know that jellyfish can't bleed? No brains, either.

Thumb saved, but after it had healed, addition of a beauty scar. He shunned the nearly severed thumb; wouldn't touch the hand. Once, while serving dinner, she "accidentally" brushed against him. He shrunk against his chair.

For an anniversary present, he insisted on plastic surgery. For her. A glossing reconstruction. Undone trauma, reminder-less skin. New skin: a graft, a gift.

He tucked her hair behind her ears, fingertips grazing her jawline, and smiled. She heard the feelings the smile imbued. Complacency, magnanimity, chivalry. She wanted to throw up the latte macchiato he'd bought her that morning. Retch the stained milk over his chinos. Instead, she left him in the waiting room and followed the plastic surgeon.

Now she drains her cup, cracked rim brushing her lips like cat tongue, a sandpaper caress. She gives love from one hand to the other, stroking the subdued scar, rolling the web of skin between forefinger and thumb. She whispers the forbidden weapons. Laugh at him. Tell him he's wrong. Blame him.

Mortify, petrify him until he questions his confidence.

If only she could birth her secret desires. Instead, she bears. What instigates an exchange? How can she kill the bearing to live the birthing?

I missed you, he says, when either returns from business. He captures her, hands and arms like webs, spindling her. She wants none: no touching, molecular interaction. No exchanged breaths. She imagines a space of her own, a square around her corpus rendered sacrosanct by four invisible, pressurized lines.

When he's over her, she wants to scream: You think I'm a tissue.

But a tissue gives more than it can take. She holds more than original intent. Her strands untwist; she parts from whole. And in the piecemeal deconstruction, she loses her entity.

She resorts to functioning without form.

What's worse: Her body disagrees with her mind. Knowing the dance, it flows and ebbs at his tricks. She loathes these moments, the primitive betrayal, the responses that contradict mindful numbness, that preclude complete discomfort. He uses her corpus against her. She enables him to set the trap. She hears the jaws close with the finality of a miner-canary's silence.

DESTINED ADDRESS

HUA

"Want one?"

Hua removed her hands from the dryer to the sound of her supervisor's approaching voice. The director of Hua's department held two circular pink pills in her palm. The pills were imprinted with smiley faces.

"It's pure, I promise."

Though Hua's hands were dry, she wiped them on her dress.

"We've an hour left of chaperoning."

"Professor Ting, you mean you want to be sober for the rest of the Fifth Annual Barrister's Ball? I offer as a friend. This never happened and will never be part of a performance review."

Laughing, her supervisor popped one and folded the sister pill into Hua's hands.

"Or perhaps you wish to save it for the return home? Spice the night up with Phil?"

The bathroom door closed in increments, fighting physics, before succumbing to rest. Hua meant to throw out the pill, but instead opened her purse. She uncapped her lip balm, reapplied, and then capped the smiling pill inside.

Back in the ballroom, she resumed her post by the open bar. A passing colleague asked about her supervisor's whereabouts, but Hua shrugged. She spent the rest of the ball discussing the Black Lives Matter movement with a Chinese student. During her linguistic contortions of Mandarin, she forgot all else. Reality revisited only when he retrieved his phone to note "we focus on supporting and empowering Black lives because they're treated as subaltern." His phone read midnight.

Forty-five minutes later, she'd helped the stumbling students to Lyfts and tidied to ease the burden on cleaning staff. During the interim

Phil had texted her: He'd be sleeping in Long Island tonight, at his cousin's house.

"Want one?" the Lyft driver asked as he rolled the windows down.

"Excuse me?"

He motioned to the water bottles in the holders by the console.

"Oh, no thank you."

They passed three green lights without speaking, letting the sirens, catcalls, street music, and arguing weigh heavy. Hua licked her lips before remembering she'd packed lip balm. She opened the cap and the bright pink pill shot out, hitting the dashboard and then bouncing into her lap. It sat there, no larger than a pencil eraser. She felt the shadow it projected. Felt its power in sound that matched the rhythm of her snare-drum pulse.

The driver acknowledged nothing. He exited onto FDR Drive, giving her ample time to recover. But Hua stayed frozen, the pink face vibrating against her thighs.

"Upper East Side your final destination?"

She could place the smiley-faced pill on her tongue. Let her taste buds stew in the smile. An expected bitter taste. Bitter, but smooth. Would it start as a hum, or emerge as a song? Murder her inhibitions and give her license to feel? Hua flipped the pill from side to side. Smile one. Smile two. Comedic side of the drama, doubled.

"Your destination tonight, ma'am?"

Snare-drum pulse beat in tandem with bright pink smile. *DestinationDestinationDestinedDestination.*

The usual address ducked under her tongue. Down the center, off the tip, out came another.

"Ah, so East Harlem."

Hua returned the pill to the cap and closed her lip balm. She shook it right to left, like reading classical Chinese. No punctuation; break by the feeling, context, and rhythm.

"Have a safe night," he said, pulling to a stop.

She stepped out. Lip balm in one hand; purse in the other. Right foot leading. Left foot following. March of stilettos and rattle of pink smile.

Past the foyer, at the buzzer.

"Hello?"

"It's me. I want to talk."

A long pause, but then the door unlocked.

Hua stepped inside, smiling pinkly.

BECAME A STRANGER TO ME

JIA

"DREW, YOU WAIT. FOR THE day. Always a day when children turn to parents. Yes, a turning on, but I mean different.

"Child turn to parent with strangeness. Strange face, voice, touch. Smelling of strange skin. Free of home smell. Many snippets of strange. Of partial turns.

"Our first argument in public, at her Barnard dorm. She close door, but her voice carry. 'I want my space to be mine! You never let me fall. You never let me break me. You hurt me by shielding me. I never want your help. Your help hurts! I want to stop hurting.' All this focus on her 'me.' My heart jerked. I call her stranger. She said? 'You've always been a stranger to me.'

"Stocks and bonds. Children are bloody stocks and bonds. Invest in your blood, in educating, teaching, hoping. For what? For why?

"All my effort. No return, but greater cost. Deeper debts. I think of little Fay, and how she listened. On rare bad days, I told her my parents wanted to return me to the dumpster that born me. She must remember her luck. I never asked for child burden. Existing's privilege. Gratitude means listening. Act your loyalty. Save your sorry.

"Harsh? She was my one child. I gave her all lives, all loves I sacrificed. I broke dam, drained river, and offered the mud. What's left? Less than nothing.

"Hua helped. And Phil. But who told her what chink meant? How harm approached? The creeping, smiling, offering, soft words of white people. Who could touch and where and why no?

"Single. Solo parent in unending marathon. I loved no one else. I worked for no one else. I killed me for her. To commit to parent, you eliminate distraction. I, me, self makes for ultimate distraction.

"You always asked for her. Right timing. After Nelson. But she fully loved your half of a brother. She chipped him into sculpture and raised him to greater height after the accident.

"I asked for privacy. I point to every family picture, every pose you suggest, and you knew your physical absence. Your words on pages, odd call when Brenda took Will and Harmony to play while you worked late...feeling the after of your help comforted me. I felt and feel. With hands, thoughts, heart. Faith looked and thinks through eyes. And we planned for you stay invisible.

"But I recognize what past. From recovering daughter, I turn to recovering mother."

WHERE'S YOUR FACE?

JIA

AFTER A DAY MASSAGING TOO many clients, Jia's hands become lobster claws. Fingers one stiff lump; thumbs hanging apart.

The skin of others absorbs her *qi*. Skin work, session after session of relearning the contours of another's body. Of targeting others' felt pain, and attempting to release in exchange for *qian* to pay statements, invoices, charges. *Qian* to help maintain a life she's never truly lived. Green for goods, for rendering of services.

She pinches her tips with the claws, fanning the bills as cramping allows, estimating the NT conversion. Even this petty cash would stretch far in Taiwan. She wonders if it's too late to return. If by leaving this adopted country, she'd regain her old young grip. Impervious once more.

She traces the paper rectangles, pulling sensation through the blind hairs on her proximal phalanges. Each bill possesses a different level of wrinkling. Different transportation experiences. From press to envelope to register to hand to wallet to hand. During each transition, exposed to different levels of care.

Some bills incurred tears. Little rips, near severs. Some were written on. "4488." "Spring." "Hold." Some are both detaching and defaced.

JIA REMEMBERS HER FIRST TIME handling American dollars. Age twelve, in her home country. Origin country. It was a wet summer day. Her mother demanded coconuts from the market. Full basket in her arms, Jia began inching home. The sky opened its mouth, throwing down its accumulated emotions. Between the slats of basket handle, she spotted a white tent.

Temporary shelter, though the color boded foreignness or death. Jia set the basket down. A man bowed in greeting. He straightened and his appendage spoke for him. *Da bi zi.* Big nose. His outfit identified his occupation: medical missionary.

"Good afternoon, young lady."

His Mandarin sounded impeccable. The right tones in the right places. White visage, but native tongue. Voice in sync with lips' movements, but incommensurate with his foreign being.

Jia nodded at the table. A spread of green rectangles, each featuring a man with a *da bi zi.* Foreign currency with foreign devils.

"Do you know the names of the Americans on these bills? I'll teach you. Like your money, ours holds different buying power. One dollar: our first president, George Washington. Two dollars: our third president, Thomas Jefferson—an uncommon bill these days. Five dollars: our sixteenth president, Abraham Lincoln. Ten dollars: a founding father, Alexander Hamilton. Twenty dollars: our seventh president, Andrew Jackson. Yes, you can touch them. Thin but sturdy, no? Smells like strength and value."

"Do Americans value their first president the least?"

"No. I suppose he's on the first dollar as the first leader. I doubt we meant to align monetary value with human worth and influence. I'm embarrassed of my uncertainty. No one taught me the history of American money...I never thought to question this. A historian would know. But most people value the personal over the historical. We live in the ahistorical. Perhaps to save face. Collective and individual face."

She had returned home, cut a coconut in half, and sipped the coconut milk Hua hadn't finished. The milk tasted more bitter than her tongue remembered. A world outside of hers existed. A world that hid from her.

THE RECEPTIONIST INTERRUPTS TO NOTIFY her he's leaving. He rotates his nose ring like he's building wisdom.

"You know, Fay told me the general story of your rift."

"Oh?" She packs intimidation into the one syllable like it's buy none get two free.

"*Ayi*, life guarantees suffering. Why actively add to that?" He taps the flag button on his shirt. "There's a pride to march to, a pride to walk from, and separate prices for both."

Jia says goodnight without meaning it.

The last one in the office, she turns on all the lights. She sprays and wipes the fibers, follicles, and skin flakes from her massage table. With her white-noise soundtrack playing, she sits cross-legged on the upper half of the table. Eyes shut, she listens to her face breathe.

She hears nothing. Lobster-claw hands to neck, chin, cheeks. She feels nothing. The feeling of lack simultaneously pants and suffocates. Its aftertaste never leaves, a haunting beyond end. Concentrated, like garlic just burned. Once helpful, now harmful.

So she reaches for the envelope of cash. Petty but powerful. It speaks to her. Jia creates a spread like the medical missionary's. Only she possesses more of each bill, and higher iterations. Faces she came to learn of after naturalizing.

Line by line, face by face. Washington, Jefferson, Hamilton, Jackson, Grant, and Franklin. American fathers and founders. Celebrated faces featured, upholding the American economy of markets and globalization and rights and most power in the world.

Again, lobster-claw hands to her immediate, moving portrait. Jia digs her knuckles into her forehead. Wanders in search of her *xiao bi zi*. No felt nose, small or otherwise. A wound where her mouth should speak. On the whole, unsaved.

From every pore drips the ooze of disgrace. On her quest to save face, she has managed to alienate and lose. Even the sawdust floating through streams of light rejects her.

She regards the long-dead-but-remembered founding faces. Straight, white, male, her former daughter would mock. Power plus privilege, her sister would state.

And Jia herself? She envies them. In the purest, basest form. Her dictionary taught her the distinction between jealousy and envy. The former involves relationships to people and/or possessions. But envy—that means unmitigated, un-extenuated desire for oneself.

Forsaken by face and family, and threatened by the world, Jia cannot imagine what lies left for her to claim. She stretches out on her massage table like a beached whale. The cash assures her: She is needed. Her clients need her for work, for hands that know how to eliminate old pain and prevent the rise of new.

Jia spreads the bills into a fan formation. Most expensive to the right, least to the left. She buries her blank, weightless face in the father faces. Green immersion. The medical missionary had spoken the truth. Thin but sturdy. Smells like strength and value.

PALLET-FORK PAIN

FAY (Looking away from the camera): One of my earliest memories is of my dad crushing my hand at the mall. At age five, because moments before a strange white woman had bent to me, face in my face, to ask me my numbers. I inserted my five fingers between us and swatted at her chin, and she scolded Dad about the ingratitude of adopted children before huffing away. Saucy with the nosies, he'd say.

(Holding up five fingers): We stepped onto the escalator, and I tried to mimic his leap of a step. I fell. My hands arrived first. As his feet came to rest, he placed his full weight onto my still-forming fingers. The weight of a grown man shocked me. By the time I found breath to cry, he realized what he'd done. He jumped aside, scooping me up, smoothing my hair, apologizing. He kissed the rim of my ear. Whispered the awkward Mandarin he'd learned. Little treasure, so sorry. No meaning to hurt you.

But he had. He'd caused me pain. Unintentionally, but the results were the same.

That's what I've got for your good intent. Take it back. Suck it in. Hold it up. Air it in the sun until petrified, burned to nonexistence.

(A beat.)

I loved my dad, especially because he only gave me seven years to love him. Some people live for glory. Rather, they live until glory kills them. Till death we ride.

(Two beats.)

Recently my watch stopped ticking. Too old to save. A regifted present from my mother. She's not going to ask for it or visit me wanting to find it on my wrist. Yesterday she mailed me a box housing all six possessions I'd kept at her apartment.

That's right: She walked the five blocks to the post office, my items probably banging around in the rainbow-striped carry-on luggage she uses for food shopping (half off at the corner thrift store—owned by a gay-pride organizer; she has no idea). Bet she rose onto the balls of her feet, bunions be damned, and asked for the smallest, cheapest box that could be shipped the slowest, cheapest way.

She means business. The amputation's complete: I'm the vestigial entity. Call me tailbone, appendix, wise tooth, plica semilunaris. Of course—she boxed me, crossed me out. Where's that checklist? Delete daughter? X fills the spot.

(Focuses lens on insignificant-seeming T-shaped object held between forefinger and thumb): My broken watch. Time undone, unmarked. Arms locked at four o'clock flat, either four a.m. or four p.m. Time of death, my mother would say. So I unscrewed the backing and opened the watch.

It's a circus in there. Cogs and levers and wheels. When working, all parts beat together to play the song of seconds, minutes, hours. The broken mechanism seemed desperately melancholy.

I researched. The piece that interests me most? The unnoticed pallet fork. This T-shaped beauty with the pink jewel pallets. In a mechanical watch, part of the lever escapement. Teamwork: pallet and lever join to stay between the balance wheel and the escape wheel. The pallet fork locks the escape wheel, negating the latter's namesake, I suppose. But at each swing of wheel balance, the pallet fork—tooth by tooth—allows for escape, for release. Adding to its multipurpose being, the pallet fork encourages the balance wheel to continue swinging, with little pushes.

This one's about the size of an ant. I promise you, my camera's flexing its zoom function. But like the ant, what unsuspected power! Remove it and one wheel escapes, while the other loses balance and swing impetus.

If family's a watch, where am I in the turning? Where am I when the turning sputters, seizes, stops? Do I wheel away or toward escape? Do I drop balance and lose drive to continue? Am I the fork, or merely its jewel pallets? Why's it even matter?

Most parents think of their childhood. The reflective ones hear their child's first scream, cut or witness cut of cord. That first touch, that curdle of love. They hold and think of raising. Of what they knew growing up. A series of avoidables and repeats.

But the self-aware parents hurt, too. Through accidents. They may apologize or they may miss the mistake, but the pain, acknowledged or missed, is irrevocable.

Children also hurt their parents. We say their worst fears aloud. We demand they recall and repent the moments they hurt us. We say, remember the time I fell on the mall escalator and you stepped on my hands and I cried? All this is code for: I know you want to forget but I won't let you; show me your guilt.

Children learn the living they endure. They memorize the way of burn marks, seared to the fourth degree. Incapable of healing, burned black. Sometimes, revisiting the increments of pain, squeezing the blackened part, they hurt with intention.

CUTTING EARLY

FAY

"THE FIRST PERSON TO INTRODUCE me to documentary filmmaking was Nelson. I knew him as my father, but Ma taught me to call him Nelson. Not one for titles or holidays, he never seemed to mind. Ma commandeered all days—we celebrated Mother's Day every day, *especially* on Father's Day. She fought for the weight that tipped the scale. He lived ungrounded, in the air. Astronaut unbound on Earth.

"Every weekend he picked me up. For 'applied learning,' he promised Ma. A true secret sets itself apart from clues, denies its own subtext. He knew how to wrap better than a snake around a branch. Asia owns no monopoly on secret weaving. We pretend we're the first, best at everything, but we know truths are universal. We just thrive on knowing what to withhold, and when.

"I think the Asians who succeed in that unexpected throat-slitting way embody the humble brag. There must be a reason for *yang guizi* and *guilao*. Unsuspecting white people in the audience—next time you travel to Asia or end up in a restaurant without an English menu, listen past the musical tones. They may bow or smile, wagging their tails for that extra tip (you know, the one you leave for 'authenticity'), but. Encoded in the obsequiousness are laughs of *foreign devil* and *ghost*. Spite lurks beneath the sunlight.

"But I did spend one Father's Day with Nelson. At age six. A year before he died, Earth grounding him in ashes. I rejected the fish balls Ma made—my first time voicing provisional distaste. She called Nelson and yelled to fulfill the anger of two parents. 'American *xiao pi hai*, brat! Eat what's served, even monkey brains. I'm sick. You take her. Day playing father. Your teaching turn.'

"Nelson seemed one of those people who knows everyone. A public figure masquerading as a private citizen. During the day, he directed ad campaigns for a fashion magazine. A *nan ting* position for a man, Ma would say. *Nan ting*, unpleasant to hear. But she meant 'vulgar, shameful.' That Father's Day, I learned what he directed off the clock.

"We sat in the four-person theatre he'd built in his apartment. He placed his S-VHS camcorder in my lap so I could learn its weight and inserted a tape into the player. Black and white fuzz; crackling. Then, in the breath of silence before Nelson's 'testing, testing,' a close-up of a white T-shirt. Across the chest, a black rectangle housing white letters in all caps: ACT UP.

"He premiered the unedited, disjointed footage with me. The clouds of people, the wasted bodies, the black and white signs. LEADERSHIP NOW! KILLED BY THE SYSTEM. YOU MAKE ME SICK. IGNORANCE = FEAR. SILENCE = DEATH.

"I enjoyed the 'kiss-in' clips and asked if the men who kissed men were brothers and if the women who kissed women were sisters. But while Ma always *told*, Nelson instead posed a series of inquiries. 'What do you think?'

"I thought no. Some were *hei ren*, Black people, and some were *bai ren*, white people. The people looked wholly different. No one like me. Cousins, I asked? 'What do you think?' I thought no. Not blood relations. 'What's a kiss?' A passing of affection from one *zui ba* to another. '*Da zui ba*, big mouth, right?' I giggled; Ma called him that. These couples appeared like *chun chi*, lips and teeth—close partners.

"'Do you think love comes to us in many forms?' I thought yes. 'Do you think people equally agree?' I thought no; I knew no. We watched the last clip. Activists staged a 'die-in' protest. They marched to the parking lot of the CDC's headquarters. They propped up their signs. And they lay down on the gravel for *jia si*, playing dead.

"What does 'protest' mean? To object or disapprove through speech or action. Act up through voice and action. Big mouth and big heart.

"The figures onscreen rose, picked up their signs, and pumped their messages in the air. But the audio cut out. Lips moving without sound, voice turned off. Lip flap. Nelson kissed my forehead, brushing against his S-VHS camcorder.

"At six, celebrating my first and last Father's Day, I realized that in the act of simplifying, we deny, we indulge in our ignorance.

"I regret asking him nothing. Asking nothing of him. Neither a demander nor a requester of attention or affection, I conformed to the active agent. I brewed questions but stored them underground, untapped, untasted.

"Who was Nelson? How did I relate to him then? How do I relate to him now? If he hadn't died by a motorcycle accident, would he have died of love? Fighting for trans rights, vets' rights, differently abled rights? Documenter of any worthy cause, questing for equal access for humanity?

"The parent who taught me to thrive in the question mark left me with the parent who dictated through full stops. If we weren't fighting, I could ask Ma. But I know better. Give me the long takes, the extended features, the director's self-indulgent cut. The covered ellipses after the period. Turn the range inside out.

"I dedicated the few possessions Nelson accidentally left me to the top drawer of my wardrobe. S-VHS camcorder. Cassette tapes. Vinyl record albums of Etta James, Smokey Robinson and The Four Seasons. A signed copy of *Angels in America*.

"A *carpe diem* man until the end, he left little behind to find. A documenter undocumented. No outstanding bills, pills, commentary, letter ashes; no ends to lead to beginnings and middles. Who did he love before Ma? During? After? I want his take.

"But he cut out early. And that's the vagary of life. We seek the simple because we know it's an illusion. It's like an old baby blanket. We find sanctuary in the baring of thread, the smell of powder and dried childhood sweat."

SHUI LUO SHI CHU: AS THE WATER RECEDES, THE ROCKS APPEAR

HUA

AFTER THE FOURTH PASS OVER with the razor, Hua failed to recognize the reflection in the mirror. Hands on face, neck, collar, breasts, ribs, hips. Surface, the feeling of a shell. Thin, waiting for the right tap to instigate the right crack—the crack whose tremor will shift the entire shell landscape, fissure upon fissure vesseling downward.

She slid her fingers through head capillaries: hair, still thick and soot black. Robe of the head. Keeper of threaded secrets.

Hold the curtain aside, tied the sides. She wielded the kitchen scissors. Parted the metal legs, then closed them. Teeth clashing, kissing, resting.

The reflected looked away, unable to save face. She fought her way, ponytail by ponytail. Right to left. A sawing, a shredding. Tail beside tail, they languished on the counter.

She needed to complete the descent into the unfamiliar. Unwrapped the razor. Hands up, raze up, she buzzed on. She listened to the blur of chattering blades. Driven by mechanics, she ploughed. Heard the sounds of finality, of falling.

With the ends peppering the sink, she whispered. Afraid and brave. Beautiful ugly.

Beneath the hair, a nightmare come true. Now, kkull unlimited, nothing remained but head surface, like an untapped egg. But also, many possibilities in this new, born state. She wanted to feel with her head, use her head like the palm of a hand. Against the mirror, a cool both expected and unexpected. Against the tile, grainy. Against the wall, bumpy. Against her discarded locks, abrasive.

Evidence of her disrobing scattered, stuck everywhere. Bits of pieces, spectrum of strands. Disjointed hair litter, reforming, clinging like static.

In the shower, she drained the remainders in concentric circles. Now, head undone, she stood so the water pelted her in concentrated shots. A series of knobby massages constructing her deconstruction. She smiled. Full with emptiness.

One butting of her towel, and a dry head. She laughed at the simplicity. At the grand stating of obviousness, like a flasher on the street.

She explored this newfound head with her hands. They told her she could pass for a Buddhist nun. With this clear head, she refracted the murky, transmitting her shine. An open head. From stunted into silence to stunner.

Shirking the temptation to clean, she let her follicle remains stand. At attention, for his arrival. Mixing of dread and happy spite. She lay her towel down in the tub and spread her naked body onto it. Upper-class skin, Ma would say while watching the servants bathe her. No field work. No mountain-people pigment tendencies. Unlike your sister.

She assumed the fetal position. Ma, she cried, what did you do to me? Worse, what did I do to you? What did we do to each other? She straightened in the tub: her birthing coffin. Hands against her peacefully beating organ. Quiet, silent, standard function. Despite every little death; every capitulation. She'd betrayed this beat, always stepping to the songs of others. And still it hummed for her continuance. True to form, true form despite her lived untruths.

A lack of color. She'd lived a life lacking color. Lonely, muted, diluted, attenuated. She'd desiccated her own flower. What were these limbs, but dried petals? This heart, but dried pistil, top to bottom: stigma; style; ovary.

The silence deafened her. Her bare head felt cold. Setting her towel aside, she closed the drain. Ran the water on hot, skin reddening. Mortification, roasting of the flesh. She increased the pressure until the faucet roared. Water at the tipping point, she turned to off. The stopping struck her with loss.

She hadn't bathed like this in years. Her best ideas used to spring from baths. She gave tribute to her losses. Cut through this woman-made lake, hands like paddles; body like a canoe. Water murmuring love.

This silence made sense. No pressures of eyes. No clock watching. Just waiting for an interruption. Because one couldn't take time. One had to steal it. In pieces of seconds, burying, hoarding like paid time off. There were hoarders whose raison d'être was the hoarding. Those who saved, and then spent it all. And those in between. Could an old flower learn to become in between?

Her skin complained in soggy collapses. The call for draining. But instead of lifting the stopper to its fullest height, she lifted in spurts, playing with levels of dissipation. A series of almosts, of false starts masquerading as success. She wanted to reconcile the insidious violence within.

Down, water, down. They said water cleansed. But didn't it also hide? Allowed for creatures of the deep to thrive. She sandwiched the stopper knob between her big toe and her longest toe. Up/down, at her will.

The water retreated, receding like her husband's hairline. Scrape, cut, raze. Enter the revelation. The uncovering of her passing. From and to: under the chin, collared bones, shouldered burdens, beaten breasts, elbowed ribs, hollow hips. If water acted the cover, then she, her severed parts, strung together by circumstance, played the rocks. A bag of rocks in limbic form. Here, her broken mind agreed with her lying body. Corpus of lies bearing, baring the truth.

There came a twisting, snapping, unhinging. He announced his arrival through floorboard protests. Bathroom door still closed, she waited. She imagined a mouth turned hole, a shriek, a wringing of lips. Floorboard protests, the vibration of stillness. The doorknob began to turn.

PREP WORK

JIA

TING XIN, FAY, LISTEN AND believe. You think at thirteen, at first blood, you know all life main points. Let me tell you, show you before others. Surely you want to hear from Ma over others. No question: I never fail you.

Art in Chinese and Taiwanese cuisine means focus energies on prep work. Prepare for cooking. Practice before performance. You prepare helpers, tools. Boards, knives, utensil beds. You line up foundations, ingredients. Garlic, ginger, scansions—*mei you cha bie*! Fine, *scall-ions*.

Cut to form. Separate. Hold knife with meaning. Blade attacks when you disrespect it. Slower! I chop fast and sure because my hands remember. You, colt hands need time. Smaller pieces, especially if you cook for *bai ren*. White people can't swallow ginger pennies like us; too weak. What *hei ren*? Stay away from them; remember the news? They cause trouble. MLK what? Know your place. Apprentice to master chef. And Ma, so double master, ah?

You fight through tiring hands. What you think I do when you sit at school? You think by hour four I tell that client, *Oh sorry, I work my fingers to point moving feels like they're exploding firecrackers*? Prepare yourself, girl, for hurt that refuses to end.

I teach you because no one will like me. You think you and Hua so alike. I tell you, she loves with convenience. *Ni kan*, how *kei ai*. Yes, she thinks you cute. The way you think of American Girls. Hold and baby for a minute there, an hour here. *Lei sheng da, yu dian xiao*. Ha! You don't know this one because of Hua. She's loud thunder but produces tiny drops of rain. You know English partner: talking cheap, no action.

Now you wash the scansions—*wo bu ting* your good English— onion by onion, once. Then together, in colander, three times. What you think that black is? Dirt from ground. Especially on white part of onion. Wash until clean. Same with peppers, spinach, spoon veggies. Especially broccoli, each bulb and between. Every produce you get from Asian stores, you must triply wash. We cheap and cut off corners. Racist? True! I know our people.

You ask for a smack? Who told you, talk to Ma like this? Hua? School? Someone you call friend? Teach me. Help me. You dare! Turn to me. Head too big for your *face*—

ARM TINGLING AS IF IT remembered delivering the blow given years ago, Jia retreated from the memory before Fay's crying began. What was the point, Jia thought, to all her teachings? All this prep work for relating. Breath before the plunge, when we attach ourselves to others, suctioning to them, squeezing tentacles around mind and heart. Are attachments ever forever? We sever these attachments. Or they sever. All that prep work, to waste. A meal dying before born into being.

CORRUPTIONS OF EACH OTHER

JIA

JIA LIVES FOR THE "I" because others have always tried to deny her. Since first blue-faced scream, she's shot down the barrel of someone else's despair. *Jia*, abode; roof and walls but no home. No one home. No one's home.

America, land of the Me First. Without child, she could've morphed into an invulnerable narcissist. But the child happened. And now that it's out and convinced of its own entity, Jia's both solipsist and mother manqué.

The man who deflated her incipient American potential stands before her. Yes, finally, here and touchable is Drew. This time she'd tangle with knowledge. They sit with their backs on the horizontal plane. They mean to enter the penetralia, but he turns and their noses meet tip to tip. Again, green beholds itself in brown; brown beholds itself in green. Decades later, in this re of the union, same and alien breed together. To revive the once, adding again.

Could she work a home into Drew's skin? One after another, like the bullets they are, her secrets zip up her throat. She swallows but there's a ratchet holding up her pathway. Bullet secrets butt each other. She refuses to open her muzzle. Grip to safety, receive his lips.

They use their limbs to draw the other's body. Point arrow toward dot. Slide to stop or start the triggered outcome. Old and new scars bleed together with the lines of age. To the right of middled, but still capable of a partner dance. They laugh at how quickly cinders overtake flame. Beneath the laughter are the wisps of potential.

Drew listens with his body. Rolls each bullet around and under his tongue. Takes in each broken, breaking word. He's a drill in her bed of rocks.

The petty longings, the dead noise of childhood, the resignation of arranged marriage. Flying for the first time. The cracks that drew the lines to the quake, to the library, to him. For a blink, taste of isostasy. Then the only test she undeniably passed positive. Baby decider. Eastward bound, to sunder sisterly connection. Coast from coast.

Jia switches without warning him of her codes. English, Chinglish, Taiwanese, Mandarin. He orients his shoulders so they're chest to chest. She emits a grounding force in a shifting, rocking world. A pull only gravitas can compel.

Without warning, flashbacks of the four men intrude again. She squeezes her eyes shut, curls up on her side, silent to his concerned questions.

What else to lose? Body still curled, eyes still shut, Jia explains the nightmare, telling him her trauma in pieces. Pieces of English are all she possesses. No. *Bu yao si.* Undo. Undo the four. Repeat to undo. Eight over four. Gun a death wave, urine like a tail-lost dog, belly Fay unmoving. To traumatize an immigrant is to pin a butterfly.

Drew weeps at this extra disrobing.

From no exposure in her native country to machine-gun waking in this *mei guo*. Beautiful country only to a select few. They say, Black trash and white recycling. The winning side mattered. Everyone in this country said winning mattered. Who is right?

Drew's smile reads hard but sad. A word she'd studied in that pocket dictionary resurfaces to sting. Ratchet, second use: "a situation or process that is perceived to be deteriorating or changing steadily in a series of irreversible steps." One-way ratchet of expanding rifts.

He hears her but in the way of hearing an echo in a cave. On his back now, his arms cradle the rear of his head. Dark hairs in his armpits glare at attention. If she touches, she'll degenerate. Voice like a starved vulture, she asks for his judgment. The silence deadens further.

She wonders if sounds ever existed outside the tree in the forest Hua used to babble about. If she's the one chained by her neck to cave wall, or if she's burnt under the sun and upon returning the tribe will flay her already peeling skin. They'll hang the strips of her hide on the wall and lay her chains down where her body used to be. Tribute to the dangers of sun flight.

Jia whispers in the formal song of Japanese. The politest, most circuitous tongue she knows. One-sided understanding, she plucks out the withering tune with a thirteen-string *koto*. A song she composes out of imagining Drew's thoughts: I'm afraid to report you're someone other than whom I hoped you were. I'm honored you chose to demonstrate your boundless self with me. I'm sorry you stand beyond reach of help, and that your stance will relegate you to passionless years of solitude without elders, parents, companions, or a child. That your quest for whiteness has purged from your mind even the concepts of sympathy and empathy. There's a problem in this room in the form of a person, and unfortunately that person is you.

Drew shifts his eyes toward her, and she reads sorrowful pity. His clement green eyes sear her. Finally, a sound. Only for her. Sound vibrating in and through her: the song of abscess stirring under skin. Larva-fly kicks, dreaming of the outside, the air and chance to rub insect limbs together. Even the shit-eating fly cleans itself. This is the sound of Jia crying.

THESE LIPS FAIL TO MATCH

FAY

CUT TO:

EXT. 123 E 7th STREET, TEA DRUNK - MORNING

FAY, hair tied back, accepts a cup of tea from a
waitress. She thanks her in Mandarin. The woman blinks
with deliberation, then smiles before returning to the
shop.

>   DREW
>   (Gripping his cup like it's
>   his buoy)
>   Bet you get that often.

>   FAY
>   (Tapping ENVELOPE on table)
>   Depends. Time and circumstance, as
>   always.

>   DREW
>   (Clearing his throat)
>   Thanks again for agreeing to meet.
>   Sorry, I'll stop repeating myself.
>   What're we drinking? Spicy.

>   FAY
>   (Pointing at a bulleted
>   point on the laminated menu)
>   Mao Feng.

>   DREW
>   Mao Feng. Described as "savory with a
>   little roughness." Apt.

>   FAY
>   (Resumes tapping envelope)
>   The menu seems a series of ponderings.
>   Maybe derived from sayings. *Mao feng*
>   *xian*. Meaning "to take risks." Soothing
>   when we encounter matches. A rarity. We

fight for titles. For that best fit. Right
peg for the right hole, all to build a
staying tent.

                    DREW
                (Nodding)
And how's work?

                    FAY
                (Stops tapping to help Drew
                clean his spilt tea)
Exactly that. And you trade stocks?

                    DREW
Someone's got to broker the deals.

SOUND CUTS OUT. A few beats of silence. For those
attempting to lip-read, syncing of words and mouths
turns from delayed to disjointed. Then Fay's and
Drew's O.S. (thought) voices take over. The dubbing's
painfully obvious. Except this is no kitschy comedy.

Fay's thoughts extend across the screen as she speaks:
He sweats like me. In films. More like underground films.
Unbeknownst to most people. Esoteric sweat.

As do Drew's thoughts: She thinks I'm a fool. Clumsy
physically and mentally. She's more articulate than Jia
gives her credit for. This is a child people would fight
to brag about. Grown child. Probably grown since first
sitting up.

Fay: Resort to weather commentary when weathered by
anxiety. He avoids my eyes. The innards of his teacup
can't be that telling. Does he believe in fortunes
told?

Drew: Will she cease tapping that fucking envelope?
Every time she hits the table it's like a descending
guillotine. The collar of this shirt might as well be a
tie. Tied tighter than the grip of guilt. No, that'd be
impossible.

Fay: I'm tempted to ask the pair next to us for a
drumroll. Where's my sequined gown? I could open with
Oscar-worthy envelope flair. Stop tapping. But what

then, with these hands? Follow his lead. Vise the tea
cup.

Drew: If I keep accepting refills, I'm going to implode
and then explode. Then she'll really be proud of me.
Accept me.

Fay: Dancing around the dance. Too much surface
that can cover. Tell me your tickings. But only the
noncontroversial ones. Give me the fiber fuzz on your
shirt. Quantify your likes. Comedy, cars? Reading,
rhyming? Favorites. Films, docs. Color, candy? Scents.
Food. Everyone needs to find a comfort in food.

Drew: Jia always complained about Fay's directness.
I NEED IT NOW. Throw me a line leading out of this
circle. Am I the only dizzy one?

Fay: What's up and down besides everything but this
conversation. A plateau unlike any I've heard. Report:
all needles dead. Repeat, all needles dead. Life
support or replacements?

Drew: Initiative. One of us must seize it. This a
test? If I do, will she blame me for suffocating her?
For leaving her no choice but the response? Like how
I followed Jia and made future-good plans without
thinking of the fucking terrible idea that would
grow, like neglected unrefrigerated mint? At first
picking, healthful and sensible and aromatic. But when
uncultivated, unasked and uncared for, succumbing to
rot?

Fay: What if he wants me to be Independent Woman? He
could fear presenting himself as Domineering Wannabe
Father. Where to start? Casual name drop. Nelson. But
what if he hated him? The trouble with minefields. Mind
fields.

Drew: Or maybe she wants me to be the Man's Man.
Intoxicated by my own masculinity. Commandeering the
unassigned role of Father Figure. That sounds wrong,
even in the walls of my head.

Fay: I hope he expects no conformity from me. Do we
regret meeting here and now?

Drew: What bladder, mind says to body. Function without. No denying; the pressure's so intense you're two blinks away from tearing up.

Fay: Regroup while he's pissing his brains out. (I've never seen someone hit tea so hard. My bladder hurts for him.) Words, where and which ones? Hands off the damn envelope. Tap tip like a knock. Tick tock like a clock. Shut up, Little Faith; thought I killed you.

They are still thinking, but now their thoughts are in imagined conversation:

Drew: Ask her. Simplest question. But also a thought experiment. Cat alive or dead?

Fay: Why're we talking about Schrödinger's cat?

Drew: I'm incorrigible. Remember why you hate parties? Right, because you're the pedantic killjoy.

Fay: A sealed box. Inside: a cat, flask of poison, and radioactive source. A laugh at the feline's expense?

Drew: She presses her palms against envelope flap. Is this parent-child dynamic both alive and dead? Open the flap to confirm the reality-bound result.

SOUND CUTS IN. A few beats of city noise. Fay untucks the envelope flap, withdraws a Polaroid picture, and slides it to table's center. Drew moves the photo so they can both see the still.

> WAITRESS
> (Addressing Fay and then
> Drew)
> *Duo he cha?* More tea?

> FAY
> (Picking up the menu)
> *Women lai kan kan.*

> WAITRESS
> *Duibuqi, wo de laoban.*

> FAY
> (Nodding)

Wo de cuo. Bu hao yi si.

                    DREW
We need to order to soothe her boss?

                    FAY
Some pressures prove universal. Choose
based on description? Nutty with a dense
mouthfeel. Or: bitter kick with a sweet
rose finish.

                    DREW
Tea drunk indeed. Fruity with a vegetal
edge? Or sweet sour of morning dew?

                    FAY
Toast with sticky rice mouthfeel.

                    DREW
Perplexing but winsome. Read no further—
that's the one.

                    FAY
Choice made.

METEMPSYCHOSIS
À LA *MOGWAI*: A NIGHTMARE

HUA

NI, YOU. THE ACCUSATION WHISTLES low, a wheezing kettle. Finger pointing white. In death she lives an opposite life. Rags trail from her skin, sagging like the party clingers she cultivated in her prime. And in this body, amalgamation of youth twisted, she's primed.

Forgive me, Ma. I'm begging you. Take the hair I shaved. I'll sew a wig for you. A nightmare is a guilt your heart confesses. The escape of regret now meeting shame. Nightmare per the *Oxford English Dictionary*: "A female spirit or monster supposed to settle on and produce a feeling of suffocation in a sleeping person or animal." Dead Ma. Which tone? Mother or horse? Mare or mother of night?

She's a *yuan gui*, ghost with grievance, possessing *mogwai* intent. No confusion here. Mama's vengeful. Invoking demon rage. Little flower presented Ma with a deviled deal. No matter if she never meant to kill.

Even without motive, the attack stops the heart. *Qi hu nan xia*. If you ride a tiger, bad luck getting off.

This Ma speaks through pulses. Hua hears through her shocked skin. *You betrayed me and my granddaughter. For this, you must eat your words, said and unsaid.*

They stand in court. The court American Supreme. Hua feels bound by a slimy gastropod. Slug? It moves. She looks down, studies it, to discover: a tongue. A stretched-long mouthless tongue. No, much worse: her *own* tongue. Living, salivating, tasting her hands without source; organ unrooted. She splits her lips to scream. No sound.

Speech needs a tongue. Yours is otherwise occupied.

The tongue lifts one end to wave. Hua searches her mouth. An empty, dry cave.

You're currently otherwise intact—according to anatomical norms. You lost your tongue because you've used it ill. Now stand at attention. Judge speaks.

Presiding over the bench? None other than Jia. Wearing a white dress. Gown of mourning. Shroud of death. She smiles against black-painted lips. Smile of the game show host. *"Da jia hao?"*

Everyone good? Hua bends her neck to rub side of head to shoulder. No external hearing protrusion. Absent on both sides. Yet she hears the court laugh.

I forgot to mention. Serpents wear no ears. Head up. Your elder sister commands you.

"Little bald flower. No curtain to hide behind."

The tongue handcuffs wriggle. Hua shudders at the fork flicking.

"What's that idiom once you taught me, clever little sister? Tied by tongue?"

Laughter screams its own name. Who play the others?

Prosecution: Ma

Defense: Dr. Morass (dressed as a mime)

Security: Phil

Jury of one: Little Fay

"All rise. And point. *Ni*, you. Repeat three more times to make deadly four."

Take your stand, pretend filial daughter. Tongue-bound hands above head. Repeat after my end. Here, I only lie in truth. Move your lips in the act. We hear beneath your sibilant words.

Little Fay stands up in the jury box, hands behind her back, reciting for yet another speech contest. "No more *dian dao hei bai*, inverting black and white. Out, truth. Truth out!"

Applause beams from the vaulted ceiling, tinkling off the Siena marble pillars. Who parrots next?

Phil the Wronged Husband. He raises his fist in the air. "We must terminate the cycle of reincarnated lies. Abort this suffering!"

Hua's detached tongue twists, shriveling at the power of tongues in cheeks.

Defense? Words of and from?

Dr. Morass shifts the beret on her head, holds her hands together like a prayer, and bows.

Content tabled. Mother's turn. *I gave my best parts to that daughter.* Jia nods as only the shortchanged eldest can. *You ate the shaved ice. She drank your drippings. The General and I raised you as the son. In you I found a developed version of my young self. You fulfilled our potential for you. But then you settled in this fool's paradise of a country and ingested the lotus they displayed. You forgot me. Sent me banknotes like I'd already become a* mogwai.

Taste the resentment steaming from your security guard. Phil only wanted to please you. Despite your stingy offerings of love. I told you at your wedding ceremony: this one worships you. Use to your advantage but reshape all ideas as his. Make him need you through infatuation and adoration. Instead? He needed you in torment, hanging over the cauldron of hope.

Turn to the child you never bore. I always wondered how a golden nugget could pop from a turtle like Jia. Wave your ribbon, Faith. You wronged her worst of all. She relied on you for recourse when my impatience or the General snapped out of Jia. But you used her for convenience. She learned from observing you. Pile wrongs to self atop further wrongs. Drink from the ocean of denial until the saltwater tastes sweet. Tastes true.

Yet these years of teaching, hiding from self-evidence hold no rights on the worst wrong. You used Faith's leap for truth to cover your fears. She knew Jia would burn the mother-daughter home. You damned her before mother blood could. To gain what? Mere stitches in your already-frayed life fabric.

Gavel gongs. Phil grunts; Little Fay claps; Dr. Morass covers her ears; Jia grins. "Ruled!"

Fay somersaults backwards out of the jury box. She paints the air red with her ribbon. The Chinese characters float toward the ceiling and remain there, verdict defying gravity. "*Zui you ying de*, guilty and deserving punishment!"

Jia gongs again. "I read your sentence with perfected English. Before you *she shen qiu fa*, abandon your body to search for Buddha's truth, you will write a *dazibao*, big-character poster. Phil, place calligraphy brush on bench. Yes, no looking surprised. You saved your hair thinking it safe from repurpose? Ma, bring us home."

You write with your tongue still wrapping your hands. You write your truths. I can only double die if you fully expose each of your selves. Shards of the flower mosaic. Release the mogwai *that hide in you, feeding on your knowing denial.*

Hua writes on skinned paper. Each formed character curls up from the page like sweet smoke. Once finished, her characters slice off a piece of Hua's wrapped tongue. A tongue for a mouth. And one for this base Hua.

Tongue behind teeth. Tongue touching mouth roof. Wagging back into commission. Hua spits the realized words. *Ni*, you. She points at Ma. Dr. Morass pats Ma's face before peeling it off. Hua judges Hua.

Yuan xing bi lu, original identity fully revealed.

NOW YOU KNOW: OUTTAKES (PART 2, DRAFT 4)

BLACK SANCTUS

Fay and Hua

Hua: Record this but promise me you'll leave it out.

Fay: Document but leave unproduced. Ultimately undocumented?

Hua: I consent to the following: audio record, listen, then destroy. I mean it, erase this.

Fay: *Ayi* Hua's terms and conditions. Why's this *sheng nu* listening? Beyond factual name, am I still your niece? One-sided interactions. Un-relatable relations. I could strip this audio before the tape begins to weave.

Hua: Stop speaking in poetics. Real, hard talk: I felt threatened by you when you came out to us. Now I need you and your recorder. Goad me into truth.

(Four beats stop a heart. Four more beats revive it.)

Hua: I've lived a holed life.

Fay: You think, *My soul is a hole*?

Hua: Maybe? I think more of unintentional loss. Like a faulty pocket. I buy all my suit jackets and skirts with pockets, or I pay for a tailor to discreetly sew them in. Purses needle me. Always assaulting my body while I'm trying to function, preventing freedom of movement. Thus, I seek deep pockets. I reject the shallow compartments of women's attire.

Fay: And in these depths, what do you keep?

Hua: Sometimes it seems the more you seek to keep, the more you lose. Typical items. Key-chained housing keys. Credit. ID. Receipts. The neglected pennies born of non-keep-the-change cash transactions. Paper scraps kept so long they've lost their meaning. Earrings I discovered were too heavy. Once, a Swiss army knife.

Fay: Only once?

Hua: When your pocket's bottom seams have frayed apart, you don't necessarily realize. You slip keepsakes in, and they fall straight through the unknown hole. You litter the city with your keepsakes. You cancel lost credit. Order new business cards. But what about the note of thanks your student scrawled on an inch and a half of school newspaper? You think about the irreplaceables. Escalate into obsessing over what you'd have kept for someone's sake. More than for someone else: for the sake of your own hope.

Fay: Ever try to recover?

Hua: No, because I know the scarcity heuristic. I thought of these mementos as irreplaceable because I kept them in the stock of one. Rarity, quantity, and time. Fear of finding and losing the one fish in the sea. But even if I managed to recover them, they would be different. Like me. I flex and flux.

Fay: You've always seemed consistent to me. Before the head-shaving, I suppose. I wanted to model you. Wear Hua Wu Ting. Heart and mind. Pretty but powerful. You killed me that day in your kitchen. "Wave your experimental *freak* flag in our faces?" You even made your sister soften in surprise. Why turn ad hominem on me?

Hua: I thought you above perfect. Thought I taught you to be, as close as humanly possible. You wounded me with your humanity. I believed I found a better Hua in you. How often I've witnessed your art, heard you echo me. What's happened to us?

Fay: I disappoint you.

Hua: Past tense. Drop the present. Wounding and healing are interwoven processes.

Fay: Disappoint*ed* you.

THE BALANCE TIPS 249

Hua: Yes, because I still believe that was an inappropriate time for your queer declaration.

Fay: Fair…point taken.

Hua: But you are still, comparatively, a woman-child. I lost my shit. And in the moment, I knew I was losing my shit, and lost it further over my own disappointments.

Fay: I get it. I'm sorry. I knew I was acting foolish too.

(Eight beats.)

Hua: I'm sorry too. Are we okay?

Fay: We're better than before. We'll get there. Will you tell me why you cheated on *Shushu*?

Hua: Oh…Phil told you.

Fay: You both seemed troubled. Erratic behavior from you, the shaved head and unaccountable time away from home; passive-aggressive comments from him. Picking fights to shut him out. I mean, your face now confirms something. Worse? Is there more? Student-instigated infidelity? No judgment. Part of a person makes no whole. People, no synecdoches.

Hua: I…let me tell you something else first. The magazines in your apartment, I left—

Fay: What?

Hua: The magazines in your apartment. You know, the magazines Grandma found. They…I…they were mine.

(Two beats.)

Hua: Read me the Riot Act?

(Two more beats making four.)

Fay: Yours. The lesbian porn magazines?

Hua: Mine.

Fay: Oh?

Hua: Yes, *my* lesbian magazines.

Fay: I get it; I get it. Yours.

Hua: The black sanctus moment. I deserve your contempt.

Fay: You think you killed Grandma. Your own mother. You can't carry that.

Hua: For a time, yes. I understand that's more of a knee-jerk emotional reaction. She may have died even without the magazines, even without...

Fay: ...her discovering your attraction to women?

Hua: Even without that.

(A beat.)

Fay: You can't say it aloud? Did you have an affair with a woman? One of your students? Don't you teach queer legal cases? I'm so—

Hua: Yes, yes, okay! Not a student, shit, never a student. I'm confused too. I'm split between established outside face and the inside one, the one I'm wrestling. It's much easier to instruct others. Hypocrisy, Fay. I have trouble accepting, let alone communicating what I feel. I fucked up and am sitting with that. Till I sort myself out. But what about us? Could we start regrouping here?

Fay: I guess. (Turns off the audio recorder.)

SCABBED THROAT

JIA

I NEVER FALL PREY TO hunter sickness. Rarely. Though I touch so many bodies, hour by hour, day after day. Much hand-to-skin interaction in massage therapy. Talk with fingers fists sides of hands. Sometimes, too, customers ask to hear my voice. Instead of rain chimes or ocean murmur or rainforest chatter. Speak in Chinese. The song of speech. Say anything.

Two weeks a cold caught me. Still holding on, too. Cough staying most obvious. I wear a surgery mask to assure coworkers and the ones who ask for my voice. But it's more than the cough. A malaise hidden. To all eyes I look usual. I feel the obscurant scabbing my throat.

The source eludes…or could be the windshield crack Hua described. A rock, flying from nowhere to ping off her glass. At first, like the cold, unnoticeable. Then: it begins with a crack.

Splitting

Cleaving

Breaking into branches. Like fruits break from trees and spring away from roots.

Cracked cracks repeat.

I wonder with the mist shrouding my head. What's life but laughing timelines? Malign, misalign, missed my lines. I remember most strange dictionary terms. Aporia. Obscurantism. Pejorism. Forget ones I read every day like Americans drink coffee. Woke with words. Now only bad ones, obsolete-use ones stick.

The answers wait under the scabs in my throat. I'm convinced of scabbing. Twenty years after former daughter's tonsillectomy (hard to even think out, ton-sill-ect-omy), former mother repeats that pain. No matter that we broke five months ago. That Ma died and so did one I called my Faith. I know her in my throat.

She hurts, I feel. She feels, I hurt. Beginning before her throat scabs, but I understood then. Child, past, present, future, lives in parents.

Age five when she had tonsil removal. I patted her shoulder before doctors rolled her to the room. Told her to behave good. That misfortune turns to blessing only if you do right. Act over talk: how to live in and out of home.

She took me too literal. Or maybe absence of swollen tissues hugging roots of her tongue frightened. No matter if either. Point: she stopped talking. Tried to touch and hear instead. Held chopsticks tighter, though she ate little. Hovered her ear to the keys when practicing piano. A week of this.

I thought she'd resume during Hua's Mandarin lessons. But she only repeated motions and mouthed words. I tried shaking her. Spill out, voice! Use tones. She never even bothered to shake left to right for no. Just watched me. Listened, deeper with each hard swallow.

Lead to water. Kick some horses, but still they close their lips at drink. So I talked double. Put her words in my mouth. I pushed smaller and larger bowls of rice porridge under her chin. Called her treasure and trash. No smile or frown. Level mouth, steady brows.

I offered *rousong*. Variations, too: pork or beef or fish floss. At the supermarket, she'd always place her hand on my calf in gentle question. When she rejected this treat, I massaged the doctor downstairs for a free check-in.

Scabbing, he diagnosed. Taking longer than usual to heal. Give time. Another week. A week gone, another massage, another check. No more white marshmallow scabs.

When would she talk again? He gave *me* look of judge, saying nothing internal or physical had stopped her. A whole speech in that stare! Easy to blame mother.

Now I cough and imagine white fluff scabbing my insides. Sealing the box of voice. I rack my throat with each expel. Sometimes they surge from my ribbed cage, and I must pause session to drink. A customer tried once holding my hand, patting my shoulder. I shrugged out of reach.

A month after the surgery, former daughter matched sound to her mouthing. She spoke of hunger. Quiet heart, but loud stomach. I placed my slippery ivory chopsticks on a bowl of cuttlefish *geng*. Watched her pick at cuttlefish again and again. Capture and accidental release. I waited.

Ten minutes of trial. She tried to demonstrate control. Accepting failure, she bowed her head, and said Ma, I need your help. What took so long? I fed her, cuttlefish never escaping. I asked her why she used tonsils to turn silent. She said: to prove she powered her voice and mouth; coordinated telling with purpose grown inside.

I wanted to slap her. But Hua told me my force meant less and more than I thought. So I cleared my throat a few times, in the way of the General. Grandfather she never met. Father I never found. But I sang my warning through shuddering of my throat. She stared, and I imagined her hands on my neck, her ears at my throat.

My coughing speaks for me. Every five minutes, little or big upheaving. Too much air inside. I need to vacuum hollows out. Suck holes up. The cancer lives in body or mind or both. I massage doctors for free check-ins. The Chinese repeats over the years even test for free. Nothing to find, they say. I must stop searching for nothing. Let nothing remain intact in its absent substance.

Do I cough for two? Cough until sides hurt. Insides, outsides. With this force, I could cough heart out of throat. Control my sounds. What inside took my power? X-ray the churning. Internal windshield crack spreading. Fissures branching into offspring, and offspring leaving origins. Heart stump. A cordless heart needs source to beat. The line on the other side to connect. Dead lines. Dull beat.

If I cut out my speech, stop the flapping of this mouth, can I turn back what I said that hurt? Can I build scabs, and cough to spit them out?

PROSIMETRIC

JIA

DEAR DREW (UNSENT)

More than one way to define a word, a life. Meaning more than
one. Same with deboning and eating a fish. You once asked me to
teach Chinese way. Is that my way, Chinese? Taiwanese? Asian? Jia
way. Learned from Jia nanny way.

You want fresh kill. Last tail flap only minutes ago. Half past death
is too late. Fresh kill breathes no foul smell. Fishy means old. If you
want a half or stripped skin, eye for bright colors. Dim means dying
second death.

But seek whole fish. They feel pain. Unite; release it in honorable
consuming.

Go home with gutted, scaled catch, example of sea bass.

In preparing for steam, cut off fins. Shear through; these limbs are
tough and take work. Search cavity and backbone for blood line. Slice
membrane. Clean blood near bone.

Remove leavings of gills, if any. No more last breaths. And we eat
the head.

Wash fish. Rinse to remind it of water, old home. Then shake off
droplets.

Naked, lay stripped fish in the coffin. Steam it to final rest. Poke
with knife's eyes, checking for solid white meat, no clarity. Plate fish
and drown with its steamed sweat. Now you season with cut ginger,
green of onions, and garlic.

Almost but unfinished. Time for sauce. Two tablespoons of sesame
oil, more ginger, soy sauce, and more garlic. Heat until bubbles burst
and liquid jumps, tribute to fallen fish. Add white of onions, toss, and
drown fish for the last time.

The fish prepared. The fish cooked. The fish ready.